Now, with the window only an inch away, Chris strove to see what might indeed lie inside. There was—

Chris lowered the inn and rubbed his eyes. Queer —it was as if there were a thick mist inside. He tried again. No, if there had ever been a way to see the interior, it was now gone; as if someone had pasted some whitish material over the inside of the window. One after another, he tried all the rest. They were all the same. You simply could not see in.

As he moved the inn about, he could hear that rattle. It came, he was sure, from a room with a single window, on the first floor. He could not be mistaken—there must be something inside.

RED HART MAGIC

by Andre Norton
Illustrated by
Donna Diamond

Fowler's Books
Buy - Sell - Trade
323 N. Euclid
Fullerton 92632
or
2634 W. Orangethorpe
Fullerton, 92634

A Tempo Star Book

Distributed by Ace Books
Grosset & Dunlap, Inc., Publishers
New York, N.Y. 10010
A Filmways Company

Tempo Books Edition 1979
By arrangement with Thomas Y. Crowell Company

ISBN: 0-441-71100-6
Tempo Books is registered in the U.S. Patent Office
Published simultaneously in Canada
Printed in the United States of America

Inside illustrations by Donna Diamond

The writer wishes to express her appreciation to Ms. Marge Geddes, the present owner of "Red Hart Inn," who very kindly permitted the use of one of her treasures for the background of this story. And she wishes to express her appreciation also to Ms. Marian Maeve O'Brien, in whose book *Collectors' Guide to Dollhouses and Dollhouse Miniatures*, the writer first came across the photograph and story of the inn.

By the author

DRAGON MAGIC
LAVENDER-GREEN MAGIC
RED HART MAGIC

Contents

RED
HART
MAGIC

1 We're Not a Family

Chris Fitton's shoulders were against the wall, his hands thrust deep into the pockets of his jeans. Behind his glasses, his eyes were half closed in a way he had been many times told was sullen.

The carpet was green and shaggy, like grass which needed a closer cutting. While it looked fine against the white-cream walls of the room, the color certainly did not match the furniture standing around on it, as if each chair, each table, and the divan would rather be in another place.

One of these chairs was just the wrong shade of green against the grass-green carpet. Another was orange, bright enough to make your eyes ache, while the divan was a mustard-yellow and along it were scattered a lot of fat cushions, each of a different pattern. After one quick glance in that direction, however, Chris turned his eyes resolutely to the two big windows, because *she* was sitting there.

Nan Mallory had planted her feet close together in a show of determination she did not in the least feel. Her hands were locked in her lap, her elbows nudged two stiff cushions which were never made to provide anyone any comfort, rather to show off Aunt Elizabeth's skill at needlework. "Aunt Elizabeth"— Nan's feeling of abandonment made her a little sick. It was not

1

her aunt who lived here; this was not her kind of place. She hated the apartment so fiercely she longed to run as fast and as far as she could.

Though where could she run to? There was not any place or anybody—now. Inside she shivered. Nobody must know how she felt—especially not *him*. She would not look in his direction. Aunt Elizabeth with her talk of brothers! They were not family at all, nor were they ever going to be! She would write to Grandma Bergman, though already she was sadly certain, that would do no good at all.

Grandma could not take her, not since she had moved to Sunnyside 'way down in Florida. She had explained it all to Nan, how you could only have grandchildren for visits there. So when Mother wrote and said—

Nan set her teeth hard together, lifted her chin a fraction—when Mother said she was going to get married again and was going to be away six months with Mr. Hawes (that is what Nan would always call him—just plain old Mr. Hawes; he certainly was not her father!) in Mexico and that Nan must stay with Aunt Elizabeth—Well, Grandma agreed just like that. As if Nan were a suitcase or something which could be sent around from one place to another! Well, they would find out! Somehow, somehow, she would go—where? There was nowhere for her to go—no old house in Elmsport any more—nothing.

Maybe she could have stood being here—just maybe—if *he* had not been here, too. Just last night he had called her stupid right to her face and said she ought to shut up when she did not know what she was talking about. Stupid! *He* looked stupid—mean, too, with his squinty eyes and his mouth set to say something to make a person want to hit him back.

Chris moved one foot an inch or so forward, pressing down a bit of the carpet grass. This was about the worst yet. Even worse than staying at Brixton two years ago over the holidays, when he was the only kid left and the teachers had to be stuck with him. Of course, he ought to be used to it by now. Only he had thought that maybe this year—when he was old enough to show some sense—Dad might just consider taking him along. Then—Chris tried to close his mind. *Her*—her and this one across the room—they certainly made a mess of things for him. Aunt Elizabeth all the time talking about being a *family!* That was certainly dumb; there was no family! There was Dad and that woman—gone off together. And there was Aunt Elizabeth and *her* here. And none of them were his family. He did not have any family, and he was not going to be pushed into even saying he did either.

If he was sure Aunt Elizabeth would not come charging in and want to know what he was doing, he would go back to his room right now. He had brought the model kit he had saved up for; he had not even unpacked it yet. Trouble was that he could not find any place in his room to work on it. He might even lose some of the parts if he opened the box and Aunt Elizabeth made him move it around. He had a couple of books he could read. But he already knew what Aunt Elizabeth thought about sitting reading—

Chris scowled. He knew what he wanted to do; and it was *not* spending the morning in here with that dummy over there, nor was it being a "regular boy" as Aunt Elizabeth kept talking about. He was a boy, and he was as regular as he wanted to be right now.

"Chris—Nan—"

Chris's shoulders twitched, and Nan's head jerked. Neither answered. Then Aunt Elizabeth was no longer in the hall but right there in the living room. Beaming as if she had invented them both, Chris thought.

She talked and she laughed all the time, as if that way she

4

could make them do or want to be what she thought they should, Nan decided. Sometimes that flood of words poured over you until you got so tired you would say yes or no without really noticing what you were answering.

"Such luck"—the bright voice rasped on Chris's ears—"tickets!" Aunt Elizabeth was waving one hand in the air like a magician who had materialized something special. "Tickets to the Disney Festival at the Rockland! I can drop you there on my way to see Cousin Philip at the hospital and pick you up at four. You see, things work out splendidly if one just does a little planning—"

Her smile looks as if it were pasted on, Nan decided. I bet she does not want us here any more than I want to be in this old apartment. If she would just let me alone—not always be pushing me around—

At the moment she refused to see any attraction in Aunt Elizabeth's treat. Disney—probably a lot of silly cartoons for little kids. But there was no escape. She would have to go with *him* just as Aunt Elizabeth planned, a whole afternoon of having to sit beside somebody who acted as if she were not real at all.

For the first time she glanced quickly at and then away from Chris. He stared at Aunt Elizabeth, his face blank. Did he always look that way, Nan wondered, as if he did not want to know anyone? What did he really *like* to do?

Aunt Elizabeth had talked on and on last night, telling them about all the things ahead. She had planned out everything—school and friends—picked out what was "best" for them both. Now, for the first time, there came a small crack in Nan's shell of resentment as a new thought crossed her mind. Did *he* hate being here as much as she did?

He certainly was not much to look at—always slouching around in spite of Aunt Elizabeth's pleas to "straighten up." His face was round, and his glasses somehow made his eyes look small; just as they always looked half closed, as if he were sleepy or so bored he could not bear to look clearly at anything. He wore that blue T-shirt which matched his jeans, and his hair was white-blond, so his brows and lashes hardly showed. He was short for his age, too, hardly any taller than she herself. There was a faded stain of paint or something down the front of his shirt, and his shoes looked as if he had been tramping through trash heaps for months.

Nan lifted her head a little more, allowing Aunt Elizabeth's words to flow over her, to face her own reflection in the mirror above the mantel. At least she looked neat. She had on the candy-striped shirt Grandma had made her and her red slacks. And she had combed her hair—which, she bet, was more than *he* had done this morning.

Her hair was a little more than shoulder-length and dark brown, and her skin was rather brownish, too. A trace of summer tan always stayed with her through the whole year. Summer—she had about lived on the beach at Elmsport. But she was *not* going to allow herself to remember Elmsport—no, she was not.

"And a clean shirt, please Chris. You cannot go out looking so untidy."

Nan smiled a little. That was telling him! And it was the truth, too. Even if she liked Chris, she would have not wanted to go to the show with someone who looked as if he had been burrowing into a dump.

"Yes, Aunt Elizabeth." He was not scowling maybe, but his voice sounded, Nan decided, as if he would like to. It was polite, but the kind of polite one heard when a person was "mad clean through," as Grandma used to say. She watched him with interest. Would that politeness crack, so he would tell Aunt Elizabeth just what he thought?

Nan was sure now that he did not care for this arrangement

6

any more than she did. But Aunt Elizabeth was *his* Aunt Elizabeth, not hers, so if anybody talked back let it be him. She herself was going to keep her mouth shut, just the way Grandma had always told her: count ten and then ten again before you answer, no matter how mad you are. Grandma said keeping quiet got a person through a lot of hard places better than letting one's tongue wag free.

For a moment Nan felt sick again. Grandma! She wanted Grandma and Elmsport, and things to be the way they had always been, before Mother stirred everything up. Mother was hardly ever at home anyway, always going off somewhere to write about a new place for *Travel Magazine*. Mother never seemed as real as Grandma, just a person who flitted in and out, always in a hurry, thinking about something else when you tried to talk about things which mattered to you.

He had gone. Probably to change his shirt. That gave Aunt Elizabeth a chance to get at *her*. Nan stiffened warily.

"You look very nice, dear."

Starting off soft, Nan believed. She looked all right, she guessed, but she was nothing spectacular.

"Perhaps there will be letters," Aunt Elizabeth continued with that brightness which made Nan so uncomfortable. "You will be so glad to hear from your mother, I know."

"Mother never writes much," Nan said flatly. "Sometimes she sends postcards. But she's busy all the time writing things that sell. Letters don't."

Aunt Elizabeth's smile appeared a little strained for a moment.

"Postcards are nice, too," she asserted too quickly.

Nan stiffened again. Maybe Mother did not write many letters, and maybe sometimes Nan wished she did; but it was not Aunt Elizabeth's place to say so, or even to think it.

"Mother won the Cleaver Award for her Iranian article last

year," she said. "That's very important. She had to go to Washington, to a big party, and it was on TV. Grandma and I watched."

"Yes, of course." Aunt Elizabeth's smile was now firmly back in place. "You have every right to be proud of your mother, Nan."

Nan looked down at her tightly folded hands. One could be proud of Mother, even if one did not know her. But she loved Grandma! If only Grandma had not decided that the house was too big and the doctor had not said she must live in a warmer place than Elmsport. Then, with Mother's getting married and all— Well, Nan was here, and she would have to make the best of it until she could figure out some way to make it better.

He had come back, and he did have on a clean T-shirt. At least it looked different, though it was the same faded blue, for there was no stain down the front. But Aunt Elizabeth did not seem too pleased.

"Chris, don't you have any other kind of shirt? I must go through your wardrobe and see just what you do need. Oh, well, at least it looks clean, and you'll have your jacket on over it. I thought we would leave early and have lunch at Magnim's on the way. This is Clara's day off, and I haven't got time to cook myself." She glanced at her wristwatch. "Chris, you run down to Haines and tell him to call a taxi. We'll be down in a jiffy."

Nan went for her own coat just as Chris, his jacket only half on, slipped out the apartment door. Aunt Elizabeth pushed at her hair in front of the hall mirror. She had on a hat which she could not seem to set at just the right angle and was frowning at her reflection.

With her navy-blue coat on and her patchwork purse in hand, Nan came back just as Aunt Elizabeth turned away from the mirror and slid into her own coat, grabbed up her shoulder bag.

8

"Come on!" she urged Nan. "Mustn't keep the taxi waiting, not with money as tight as it is."

They went down in the self-service elevator, which Nan had hated from the first. It made her feel as if she were caught in a trap. She almost held her breath as she watched the light flicker along the numbers above the door until they stepped out into the lobby.

At home Nan had never become so upset over little things. But then there everything was familiar, and she felt safe. Here where everything was new and so different, she would rather stay in than go out.

Chris stood outside next to the big doorman. There was the taxi Aunt Elizabeth had sent him to order. He glanced right and left along the street. Why could they not walk? Aunt Elizabeth always took cabs; then the cabs got stuck in traffic. You would really save time by walking. Also there were the stores—

He wondered if there was a shop that sold model kits near here. Dad had sent him—he felt in his pocket, and his fingers crooked around the bill he had rolled up. It was more than Dad had ever given him before, as if he was— *Was* Dad trying to make up in that way for dumping him on Aunt Elizabeth? Anyhow it was Chris's own money, and he would spend it just as he wanted to this time. He would pick out something really super; when he saw it, he would know. That is, if he ever got a chance to go shopping. So far Aunt Elizabeth had laid down the rules, and at first he would have to do what she said; at least until he learned more about this place.

"Here we are!"

Involuntarily Chris's shoulder hunched as Aunt Elizabeth's gloved hand tightened there.

"Thank you, Haines," she said as she swept Chris after Nan to the waiting taxi.

Magnim's was very different from the hotel where Grandma had twice taken Nan for Sunday dinner. There were tables in a big room, and a lot of conversation—a roar of sound. Aunt Elizabeth did not let either of them look at the menu and make their own choices. As if they were babies, she did the ordering in a firm voice. Nan picked at salad with a dressing which smelled funny and tasted even queerer, turning with some relief to a chicken sandwich. Luckily there was ice cream afterward.

Chris ate slowly, chewing as if he were counting the number of times his jaw must move up and down. Aunt Elizabeth fidgeted and kept looking at her watch.

"Chris," she said at last, a fraction more sharply. "You must finish. We shall be late. As it is, I have to drop you off at the theater and get on to the hospital. And, remember, you are to wait in the lobby when you come out, unless you see me there already. With traffic as it is, I might just be delayed."

Deliberately Chris drank the rest of his milk. "Yes, Aunt Elizabeth," he answered.

It was when the taxi drew into the other lane so they could pause in front of the theater that Chris saw the red sign which was too big to be missed. Salvation Army Store! One of those! Once more he fingered the bill in his pocket. Last year he had discovered the treasure house that sign meant. All kinds of things were sold there. Why, he had gotten five books—good ones—for a dollar, and a transistor radio, old but fixed up so it ran fine. Then there was the time he discovered a box of all kinds of shells. Somebody had mounted them on cards with their names printed under them.

He shot a glance at Aunt Elizabeth. She was looking at her watch again. They must be pretty late. If he could just—

The taxi pulled to a stop, though the meter still clicked busily. Aunt Elizabeth opened the door with one hand and shoved the tickets at Chris with the other.

<a>.</a>

.

"Go right in. It must be just starting, so hurry. Remember, stay in the lobby until you see me."

"Sure," he agreed. Then he was standing next to Nan, and the taxi had again swung from the curb.

Chris held out one of the tickets in *her* direction.

"Here," he said shortly, "you go on in."

"Aren't you coming?"

To Chris this was too good a chance to miss. There was no telling when he might be able to get out alone again.

"Not now," he answered curtly. "You go in."

Nan made no move to take the ticket though he tried to press it into her hand.

"What are you going to do?" she demanded.

"Don't be so stupid." His temper flared for an instant. "You go in. It's none of your business. Now is it?"

Slowly she shook her head. "But Aunt Elizabeth—"

"Go on!" He wanted to push her through the door. Throwing Aunt Elizabeth at him that way—

"All right!" Nan took the ticket.

Chris waited only long enough to see her reach the outer door of the lobby; then he turned and was gone, back up the street. Nan opened the door and let it close again, with her still outside. Chris was up to something. She had no intention of meekly going in to watch Disney, not now. She was going to see where *he* went and learn why.

2 Bargain Counter

Luckily Chris did not look back, so Nan did not have to dodge into any shop doorways but could trail him openly. Then he did turn to look into a big window. She caught a glimpse of the sign up above: "Salvation Army." What in the world was Chris doing going in there? She scuttled ahead, not really understanding why she must follow him, but knowing that somehow it was important.

As she, in turn, peered through the big window she could only see the mass of things on display: furniture, a baby crib, a lamp. What did Chris want with old things like these?

Nan's curiosity was so aroused that, in turn, she dared to go inside. It was rather like a discount store, only a lot more crowded. There were three women by one counter. One of them kept reaching down to measure dresses against a little girl with a runny nose, who whined she wanted to go home. Another woman was pushing and pulling apart coats hung along a big rack, fingering their material and looking at the tickets pinned to their sleeves.

But where was Chris, and *what* had he come here for?

No one seemed to be paying any attention to her. Nan sidled by the women at the dress counter, moving toward the back of the store where Chris must have gone.

There were counters here like in a real shop—cases with transistors, and toasters, a couple of boxes with jewelry lying on dark cloth in them, while on the tops of the cases balanced some handbags, beyond them some cups and saucers, each with a different flower pattern, a number of belts. Then she caught sight of him and stopped by the belts.

Chris was busy at a big table where there were piles of old books and magazines. Some of those were tied up in bundles with price tags stuck under the twine which held them together. Those he pushed aside to look at the books.

He thumbed down the line of volumes. There were some how-to-do-it books, but just about gardening and stuff like that. Nothing really useful. Old story books with the lettering on their backs so dim you had to look really close to read the titles—nothing but Hardy Boys and things he had already read, like *Tarzan* and *Huckleberry Finn*. Somehow Chris felt a strong disappointment. It had been so easy getting here, as if he were meant to find something really good. He pushed another pile of *National Geographics* to one side. There was only a battered *Tom Swift*—kid stuff.

As he worked his way around the table, Chris's frustration grew. But he *would* find something; he was determined on that. Now he moved to the next big table. Toys—there was part of a railroad set. Not much good unless you had more pieces; anyway he did not care for trains. Two Panda bears, and a whole row of dolls. A pile of jigsaw-puzzle boxes caught his eye, and he glanced at the cover pictures. No good. Not when he had no place he could start a puzzle and just leave it out. Turn up with one of those, and Aunt Elizabeth might ask questions.

Impatiently he pushed past the toy table and reached the glass-fronted case at the very back of the store. Guns—old guns—and a sword! Again he realized there was no hope of ever keeping such a secret in the apartment.

There were some plates, cups— Oh, these were the antiques, the old things people collected. He lingered before a set of dull-surfaced coins laid out carefully on a strip of threadbare velvet. But he did not know anything about coins. There was a box of stamps all thrown together—

Chris knew what he longed to find, a buy so different that it would make this stay with Aunt Elizabeth worthwhile. He *had* to find it!

"Looking for something, son?"

Startled, Chris glanced up at the man standing behind the case. He was smiling but watchful. Maybe they watched all kids in here, thought they might grab something.

"Got any model kits?" He asked to prove that he was a prospective customer and not a shoplifter.

"Model kits? Let me see." The man went to the wall shelves where there were boxes piled. Chris moved farther along the case. Beyond the box of stamps were three daggers laid out, one with a silver hilt. Chris regarded them longingly but knew he had no chance of getting one of those. That man was not going to sell him a knife, not even if he could afford it.

Beyond the daggers was something else. At first glance Chris thought it a dollhouse, but a very small one. He would have passed over it, except there was something about it— He had never seen a house just like it, except in a book once. And that picture flashed into his mind. It was not a dollhouse. It was the model of an inn! There was the high arch of an entrance, flanking the smaller door; that was where the old coaches drove through to an inner courtyard. The upper part of the building was a cream yellow with broad dark beams across it in an angled pattern. The tiny windows had threadlike markings on them, dividing their glass into bits of panes, diamond in shape.

"Here you are, Columbus's flagship, and a World War II bomber—"

Chris hardly heard what the man said as he slid two boxes onto the top of the case.

"That"—he pointed at the inn—"What's that? A dollhouse?"

"That? Oh, you mean the peep show."

Chris did not take his eyes from the inn as he asked, "What's a peep show?"

"You look in the windows, see?" The man slid open the back of the case after he had unlocked it. He lifted out the inn and put it down before Chris. "It's old, that. A real unusual piece."

Chris fumbled for his money. "How much?" he demanded without taking his eyes from it. He knew he had found what he had come for, something which would be his, transform this stay with Aunt Elizabeth into a period of time he *could* get through.

"It's not a toy." The man sounded impatient. "Not now anyway. It's an antique."

"How much?" Chris repeated doggedly. If Dad's gift was not enough, he would get the rest somehow. He had to have that! It was different from any model he had ever fooled around with, and he wanted to take it up in his hands, look through those tiny windows, just feel it.

"Ten dollars." The man's hand had already closed upon the inn. He was going to put it away again as if he were very sure that Chris did not have ten dollars.

"I'll take it." Chris brought out his bill, smoothed it flat. "See, I have the money, more than enough. It's mine," he added, guessing what the expression on the man's face meant now. "I had a birthday," he improvised—no use going into the facts of why Dad might have given it to him—"It's a present, and I can spend it on anything I like."

For a moment the man looked from Chris to the crumpled bill and then back again. Chris must have sounded convincing, for at last he nodded. Then he reached for a box and carefully slid the inn into it.

16

"Come up to the cash register, son." He did not give the box to Chris; rather, he carried both it and the money as if he expected some difficulty over the sale might still arise.

Nan had just time to dodge behind a rack of suits as Chris turned. He had bought something. But what? And he seemed different somehow, as he passed without seeing her, as if he had found something exciting. She wanted to know what made him look like that, so different from the sullen boy who had ignored her and made his dislike so plain.

She squeezed along behind the racks and by the counters on the other side of the store. Luckily Chris never looked in her direction, and she was able to reach the door and get out before he moved away from the cash register.

Surely now he would return to the theater, and she did not want him to know that she had followed him. She trotted back to the lobby but did not pass the ticket-taker. If Chris did not come, she would not go in alone.

But he did come. Only when he saw her sitting on the bench, he scowled. "What're you doing here?"

"Waiting for you." She hoped her voice sounded just as snappy as his. "I'm not going in by myself."

"All right, I won't make you."

He had the box under his arm, hugging it close to him. Now he marched straight past her, holding his ticket in one hand and heading toward the inner door.

Nan got up quickly and got out her own ticket. She wanted to tell him she knew where he had gone and to demand to know what he had in the box, but better judgment suggested that she keep her mouth shut. She was sure Chris was not going to answer any questions now.

He did not even wait for her, though she was certain he knew she was following him, but walked firmly on into the dark of the theater where the sound track was loud with rolling thunder. Nan trailed behind, her irritation growing with every step.

Surely when Aunt Elizabeth came, she would notice the box and ask questions. But later, as they emerged blinking into the lobby, Nan did not see the box. There was, she decided after a critical survey, a bulge in the front of Chris's jacket. What did he have to hide from Aunt Elizabeth?

Chris himself was faced with just that problem. He had wrapped the box in his scarf and left it under the seat, positive during all his efforts to disguise it that Nan was going to ask him what in the world he was doing. He had had the words, "Mind your own business," on his lips all the time he worked to conceal his purchase. But Nan, caught in spite of herself by the story on the screen at that moment, had apparently not been aware of what he was doing.

He could not quite understand why he felt he must keep the inn a secret. There was nothing wrong in spending the money Dad had given him for something he wanted. Aunt Elizabeth might try to make something of his leaving Nan and going into the Salvation Army place. But he had not been told *not* to go, and after all, he was old enough to do something like that. Yet from the first the inn had seemed a secret which he did not want to share with anyone else. Peep show, the man had called it. Chris had had no chance to peep into the windows— What *was* inside? He was hot with impatience to get home and see.

Aunt Elizabeth was late, of course. Nan sat at one end of the lobby bench, and he at the other. And Chris was so filled with his need for secrecy he did not even notice she kept watching him.

Chris had that thing, whatever it was he had bought in the store, stuck under his jacket. Nan tried to guess from the lump what it might be. There had been a million things, maybe even

18

more, for sale in that store. So what *had* Chris bought from that counter 'way at the back? Not a book, because he had looked all over the book table and then gone on.

She had seen the toys on the other table, but he had not stayed there either. The case at the back— She was sure there had been guns there. A gun! Had Chris bought a *gun?* He would not dare, and she was sure that the man would not have sold him one either. So—

"I *am* late!" Aunt Elizabeth's voice caught Nan's attention. "I'm sorry! But Cousin Philip wanted me to make some phone calls for him, business matters. Come on—there's a taxi waiting. I stopped at Fung-How's and got us a Chinese dinner. That will be fun, won't it? And how was the show?"

She rattled on, urging them before her into the taxi. Aunt Elizabeth's life, Nan decided, was made up of waiting taxis. There were some big boxes on the seat giving out smells which Nan found queer; probably these contained the Chinese dinner. She shoved them aside and settled into the far corner. Chris sat down carefully, one arm up near his chest. He was holding that thing. Would Aunt Elizabeth notice?

"How did you like the Disney pictures?" Aunt Elizabeth repeated her question in a new way.

"All right," Chris returned without enthusiasm. He wanted nothing but to get back to the apartment as quickly as possible. If he had any luck at all, he could then reach his room and hide the inn (he would have to find somewhere good for that) before Aunt Elizabeth spotted that he carried something.

"It was fine." Chris was surprised when Nan spoke up. "The second picture was better—" She had seen all of that, while the first one had been something of a muddle because they had missed part. Now she remembered her manners; too belatedly, she knew. Grandma would not have been pleased.

19

"Thank you for the tickets, Aunt Elizabeth." She rather stumbled over the "Aunt Elizabeth" part. "It was good of you to let us go."

"I am glad you enjoyed it, child." Aunt Elizabeth smiled. She might be waiting for some answer from Chris, too. But he was staring straight ahead and said nothing. After a glance at him, Aunt Elizabeth's smile narrowed a little. "Watch out for that carton, Nan. We don't want Egg Foo Yong all over the floor, now do we?"

Nan obediently steadied the carton, sniffing at the odor from it. She could not yet make up her mind whether she wanted to try Egg Foo Yong—whatever that was—or not. Mostly she and Grandma always had things one knew, vegetables and fruit from their own garden, meat from the butcher's. Grandma didn't like what she called "fancied-up" food.

A drizzle began just before they reached the apartment-house door. Aunt Elizabeth spoke sharply when Chris did not reach for his share of the boxes. And for some reason she could not understand, Nan herself took two, leaving him only one. He ought to be able to manage that, even holding on to whatever he had inside his jacket. Aunt Elizabeth lingered to pay the taximan, but Haines held the door open for them to hurry through.

There was the ordeal of the elevator; then Aunt Elizabeth used her key, and they were back in the apartment, carrying the cartons through to the kitchen. Chris set his down with a thump on the table and was gone before Nan could turn around.

She went to her own room to shed her coat and head scarf. Only this was not *her* room—its tidiness made it Aunt Elizabeth's, not Nan's. All which really belonged to her was the picture frame—the double one—on the dressing table. One half of that was Grandma, taken last summer out by the big white rosebush. The other was the picture of Mother from the Cleaver Award Dinner—Mother who never was at home in Nan's room the way Grandma fitted in.

Nan looked at Grandma now. A feeling of loss came over her. She blinked twice hastily. If she was silly enough to cry, Aunt Elizabeth would want to know why. Think of something else—quick! Think of Chris. What had he brought back and mean to keep a secret?

Chris pulled his suitcase out from the closet. He had set the inn carefully on the bedside table. Luck had been with him all right. He had fully expected Nan to blurt out about his leaving her alone. But she had not. Only briefly, he wondered why. A good hiding place—this suitcase—was all he could think of right now. He tucked the inn into one corner, using his old hiking shirt as a cover. Aunt Elizabeth had already told him there was no wearing *that* around here. He did not even have time to peek into the windows. But there was one thing; when he picked up the inn to put it away, he heard a rattle inside. So he was extra-careful covering it up and returning the suitcase to the closet. Maybe part of the inn was broken. He would have to wait until he had a chance to really examine it. If it was broken, he might be able to fix it.

"Chris—Nan—"

Supper! Chris gave a last push to the suitcase, sending it up against the back wall of the closet. He would have to watch that Clara did not move it around too much when she was cleaning. Clara was pretty energetic when she dusted and swept. Aunt Elizabeth did the good china and things herself; he noticed that last week. It was one reason why he had not started in on the model. Let Clara move one of these once or twice and probably nothing would be left.

21

Nan was already in the kitchen when Chris slouched in, wearing his usual indifferent expression. She did not glance at him as she set out plates and silverware. Aunt Elizabeth told him to get the milk and fill their glasses. He had discovered that Aunt Elizabeth believed a boy should make himself useful in ways Chris did not think at all suitable. But there was no use fighting over it. He banged shut the fridge door, and went to get the glasses from the cupboard while Aunt Elizabeth dished out a mixture of stuff from the cartons.

"Just home in time," she observed as a gust of wind and sleet beat against the window of the small kitchen. "This is going to be a bad night. All right, we're ready now—"

Gingerly Nan tasted the small pancake-looking things Aunt Elizabeth called Egg Foo Yong. She decided that they were not bad, just strange, and she was hungry. There was a sauce to dabble over them—salty—then a brown rice with what looked like little bits of ham cut up fine, as well as a portion of what Aunt Elizabeth called "Chicken Chow Mein." Nan ate steadily. Chris was cleaning up his plate, too. Though he never raised his eyes from that. It was as if eating was a business, a job one had to finish as quickly as possible. Only he need not think he was going to slide out and leave her with all the dishes. Aunt Elizabeth had said this morning they must take turns washing and wiping when Clara was not here. Nan watched narrowly for any sign Chris meant to get out of the job.

Aunt Elizabeth was talking, talking. Mostly about this Cousin Philip who meant nothing to Nan—though, of course, he was Chris's kin. It seemed, however, that Chris did not care about him either, even whether he was in the hospital or not.

The flow of words only stopped when they had fortune cookies. Nan smoothed out her strip of paper to read it: "What

22

the eyes see not, the heart craves—" She repeated the words aloud.

"Hm"—there was an odd difference in Aunt Elizabeth's smile—"What is yours, Chris?"

"Silly stuff! 'Clear conscience never fears midnight knocking,'" he half-mumbled.

"Good sound advice," Aunt Elizabeth said. "Now I have to make a long-distance call. You can go ahead with the dishes. And, Chris, see the rubbish all gets down the hall to the incinerator tonight."

"Yes, Aunt Elizabeth," he replied, crumpling his fortune and throwing it into the emptied carton that had held the Egg Foo Yong. But Nan wanted to keep hers and think about it, even though she did not quite understand what it meant.

3 The Red Hart

Sunday at Aunt Elizabeth's was different, too. They went to church in the morning, Aunt Elizabeth seeing that they were both dressed as she said "suitably." This church was a large one where people did not seem to know even those who shared the pew with them. Nan missed the friendliness of Grandma's church. Chris sat stolidly, as if all were an ordeal to be endured.

But the afternoon was even worse. They had dinner in another big restaurant, and then Aunt Elizabeth summoned one of her ever-helpful taxis and carried them off to the park, where there was a zoo, a lake, and other supposedly interesting things. Chris dragged along so far behind that Aunt Elizabeth was plainly annoyed when she turned for about the tenth time to see where he was.

Nan watched a black leopard. She felt sorry for it because the animal was never still, pacing back and forth in its cage as if it wanted to be free. She did not like the big apes at all; one of them made faces and spit at people who had stopped by the cage to watch. But the birds were beautiful with their many colors and plumed tails; and there were two lion cubs, who were rolled up together on a blanket, asleep like kittens.

Her feet began to ache, and she was glad when Aunt

Elizabeth took them into a place where Coke and ice cream were sold and they could sit down for a while. It was then that Aunt Elizabeth met a friend by the cash register and told them to run along and find a table and wait for her.

For the first time that afternoon, Chris spoke directly to Nan. "She thinks we're little kids!"

He shoved his dish of ice cream with dangerous force off the tray he was carrying. Nan was just in time to save it from crashing to the floor. She pushed it back in his direction. "I guess she thinks we like such things. Maybe she doesn't know."

Chris glowered at the ice cream, digging a spoon into it as if striking back at the world. "I'm not about five years old," he exploded. "The zoo, for pete's sake! The zoo, yet!"

"The birds were nice." Nan licked at a spoonful of hot fudge sundae. "I didn't like that monkey though, the one who spit at people."

Chris grinned crookedly. "That ape had the right idea. Why not spit at a bunch of dumb people come to look at you shut up in there? I don't like to see animals in cages—not ever."

Nan found she could agree with that, remembering the leopard.

"But they're all being killed off. If any are to be saved, they'll be in cages."

Chris shook his head vigorously. "Don't have to be in cages. You never saw Lion Country, I guess. They have them outside there, free. They walk right across the road. You can drive through in a car, but you have to keep your windows shut and go real slow."

"When did you see that?" Nan asked.

"Last year. I went to Florida with Butch Wilson and his folks. We took some camera shots. There was one old lion sleeping there as if he didn't care about anything. And in the next section

25

we had to stop the car 'cause a mother antelope was feeding her baby—right in the middle of the road. None of them were shut up in cages there."

"My grandma's in Florida," Nan announced. "When I go to see her, maybe we can visit your Lion Country."

"You used to live with her. How come you didn't go to Florida with her?"

Nan carefully used her spoon to combine fudge sauce with ice cream, pretending to study what she was doing.

"Didn't she want you around any more?"

Now she raised her eyes to answer hotly, "Of course she did! But Dr. Simmons said she had to go and live where it was warm. And the only place she could afford was Sunnyside Retirement Acres. They don't like children there—you can only visit. Then Mother got married."

Chris's face turned blank. His mouth was again a sullen line. "Yeah, they got married," he said flatly. "And you had to come to Aunt Elizabeth's to live. You don't need to go into that."

"I didn't ask to come here!" she flashed. "She's not *my* aunt."

Chris shrugged. "Kids always get shoved around, until they're big enough to do something about it. No use trying before then."

"What do you plan to do?" Nan inquired. She did not want to think ahead to a long time of being shoved around until she was old enough to take measures to make her own life. She did not even know now what kind of a life she really wanted.

Chris stared down at the table top. "It doesn't matter—not now."

It was as if he had pulled down a heavy curtain between them. Nan went on spooning up her sundae. Chris had never really talked with her before, but their exchange had not lasted long. He must hate living with Aunt Elizabeth just as much as she did. Nan wondered how he had lived before. Did he have someone

like Grandma, too? She longed to ask, but she did not quite dare.

"There you are!" Aunt Elizabeth swooped down upon them. "That was great luck, Nan. Mrs. Ames is driving Martha to school tomorrow and will stop by for you. I really didn't want you to go off alone the first day. It will be such a change from Elmsport to the Wickcoff Grammar School. It's all arranged; they will be by for you at eight fifteen. Chris can ride along, too. They'll drop him off at the Academy as they have to pass right by there on the way."

Aunt Elizabeth had a cup of coffee, which she now sipped. She made a face. "Bitter—" She pushed the cup toward the center of the table. "No one in these places seems able to produce a drinkable cup of coffee." If she caught the look of dismay on Nan's face, the deepening of the sullen droop of Chris's mouth, she refused to accept either as criticism of her own plans for their welfare.

It was not until after supper that Chris was able to get to his room by himself. He hesitated by the closet door. Get the inn out now? That was what he wanted. Yet the feeling that it was his alone, that he did not want anyone else to know about it, kept him from reaching for the suitcase. At last he sat down on the side of his bed. Aunt Elizabeth, that girl—they had to go to bed sometime. Then he could use his flashlight, get a good look at what he had bought. He squirmed unhappily, impatient to get at his find.

Mostly he did not want to think about the Academy tomorrow. Just because Dad had gone there, he was now supposed to enjoy it, according to Dad and Aunt Elizabeth. But the truth was that he hated the place.

Chris took off his glasses and rubbed his hand across his eyes. Could he help it that he was so nearsighted he was not good at sports? Twice he had broken his glasses back at Brixton trying to play basketball. He could never see why chasing around a ball, any kind or shape of a ball, was so important.

And if a guy liked to read or knew what the teacher was talking about, then he was a soppy square or something. Chris rubbed his forehead again. Al Canfield had threatened to give him the "business" if he outsmarted Greg Fellows in class once more. Simply because Greg was team captain, and Chris had refused to write his themes for him.

Chris's round face took on a stubborn cast. He was not going to be their tame theme-paper writer, doing just what they said, as Perry Winn did in Chemistry. He supposed they would get him for it tomorrow when he did not produce the book review for Greg to copy.

Kids were like the animals at the old zoo. They were all in cages. Maybe you couldn't see the cages really, but they were there. He had always thought that when he was older Dad would see that he didn't have to be caged up. Chris pounded one fist on the bed.

"Chris?" Aunt Elizabeth's voice was right outside the door.

He got up quickly and went to answer.

"There is the special on TV—the one about Africa."

Chris opened the door. "I've got my book review to write," he said shortly.

"Why do you leave your homework until the last minute?" Aunt Elizabeth asked. "Well, I suppose I should be glad you do, do it. Margery says she has to keep after Tim every minute to get him to turn in anything at all."

But she was studying him more closely than usual, and Chris felt just a little guilty at the lie. Only a little guilty, however, not enough to send him to the living room to watch TV with the others. He closed the door and stood listening. Yes, there was the sound of the TV being turned up. But he'd give them just a little more time. He had forgotten all about this show.

When he could be reasonably sure both Aunt Elizabeth and Nan were listening only to the show, he burrowed into the closet, drawing out the suitcase. He sat on the floor, his back carefully between it and the door, ready to slam the suitcase back into hiding should anyone come.

He shook off the old shirt and brought out the inn, carefully cupped in both hands. It was even more perfect than he remembered it. He had made many models, and quite difficult ones, but this was a work he was sure he could never equal.

A peep show, the man had said. You looked into those tiny windows, and what did you see?

Slowly Chris lifted the inn, so that the largest of the diamond-paned windows was at eye level and brought the whole of the small house close to his eyes.

But his glasses—those were in the way!

Hastily he swept them off and laid them on the bed. If he held something very close without them, he could manage all right. Now, with the window only an inch away, Chris strove to see what might indeed lie inside. There was—

Chris lowered the inn and rubbed at his eyes. Queer—it was as if there were a thick mist inside. He tried again. No, if there had ever been a way to see the interior, it was now gone; as if someone had pasted some whitish material over the inside of the window. One after another, he tried all the rest. They were all the same. You simply could not see in.

As he moved the inn about, he could hear that rattle. It came, he was sure, from a room with a single window, on the first floor. He could not be mistaken—there must be something inside.

Warily Chris turned the inn upside down to inspect the smooth piece of wood which formed its base. He could not see any nails or screws there. But there must be a way to open it somehow, the boy was sure of that. Maybe it was a trick—like a Chinese-box puzzle he had once seen. Only he must be very careful in trying to solve it; he did not want anything to break.

Longingly he thought of the small tools he used for model building. Dare he try to pry off the bottom? No. Maybe if the inn was very old, the wood itself would split. He would just have to solve the puzzle some other way.

With regret he returned the model to his suitcase, shoved that back into hiding. He began to undress. Aunt Elizabeth didn't approve of reading in bed. But he could; at least until the program was over. Chris had discovered long ago that if you had a problem and could put it out of mind for a while, then when you thought about it once more, sometimes you saw the solution.

Nan watched a big-eared elephant squirting water over its baby. Chris said animals ought to be free, as this one in the picture was. She tried to think only of what she was seeing and not of tomorrow's trip to school. Chris was lucky. He had been here a month, had had time to learn what he had to do, to meet the other students. She was starting late in the term and that would mean she would have an awful lot to make up. City schools were different from those in Elmsport. They must have a lot harder subjects. And she did not know anyone at all. She hated going into a new room, having everyone look at her as if she were as different as the strange bird now stalking across the TV screen.

She felt rather sick, and she was going to have a headache, she was sure. Not that she would try to beg off from going tomorrow. Grandma had always said there was no use trying not to face things; that only made them worse. Though Nan could see nothing really worse than what was going to face her tomorrow.

She did not eat much of her breakfast on Monday morning, though she did drink her orange juice, which was the only thing that tasted good. The toast was too dry, in spite of the marmalade she spread thickly over it. Such bites as she swallowed rasped her throat. She got down about three spoonfuls of oatmeal, and envied Chris a little. He ate with his usual slowness, though Aunt Elizabeth told him twice that it was almost eight five and they must not keep Mrs. Ames waiting.

He was still at the table when Nan excused herself and went to get her coat and cap, being sure she had the envelope with her transfer grades in it. By the time she was back in the hall, he stood by the outer door, plainly impatient, bumping a book bag against the wall as if he would like to hammer it clear through that surface.

Mrs. Ames waved to them from her car as they came out of the lobby. Nan hurried forward, not out of eagerness but because she felt she had to get the worst over as soon as possible. She saw another girl in the back seat.

"This is Martha, Nan," Mrs. Ames said. "You two can ride in the back. Chris can get in the front as he gets out first."

Nan managed a "Hello," and Chris echoed her in his I-don't-care voice. He ignored the girl. Nan glanced at Martha, who eyed her in a way which made Nan feel that either her hair was dreadfully untidy or else she had spots on her face.

Mrs. Ames said nothing more. It was plain she was concentrating on making her way through the early-morning traffic, a rush of cars which made Nan wonder how anyone dared try to edge into lines such as these.

Nan wanted to break the silence at first, needing desperately to have some small token of acceptance from this stranger. Then pride came to her rescue, and she sat looking straight at the back of Chris's tousled head. All right, if this Martha did not want to talk, she could be quiet, too.

"What grade are you in?"

When abruptly Martha did ask her that, Nan was startled. "I'm in the sixth—I was in the sixth," she corrected herself.

Who knew where she would end in the new school, especially coming in at the middle of the term?

"Then they'll probably put you in the Crab's room." Martha sounded smug. "I'm in Miss Hill's. But we're full—they can't get anyone else in." Her voice held a note of pleasure as if she were only too glad to impart this daunting bit of information.

"Who is the Crab?" Nan asked, refusing to be put down.

"Miss Crabbit. She's as old as the hills and twice as hard—that's what my friend Ruth says. She really piles on the work. Ruth got her mother to transfer her out of that class in a hurry when school began."

When Nan made no reply, Martha continued, "She won't like you coming in in the middle of the term either. If you can't keep up, she'll put you back at grading time. She did that last year to a couple of the kids."

The car pulled to a stop, and Chris got out in front of a tall brown building, which was set back from the street a little, with an iron fence between it and the sidewalk. He looked around at Mrs. Ames, still ignoring Nan. "Thanks for the lift."

But, Nan thought, he did not sound as if he were thankful at all. She watched him, turning her head as the car moved out into traffic again. He was walking with his shoulders a little hunched, almost as if he hated what lay ahead of him.

She had envied Chris. Now she began to wonder if he liked the Academy. He looked so—so as if he expected something unpleasant. There were boys in the yard, but Chris did not look at or speak to any of them, not as long as she could watch.

"He's your brother now, isn't he?" Martha demanded.

"No!" Nan was quick to deny any relationship with Chris.

"Your stepbrother then, or something like that. Didn't your mother marry his father?"

"Yes," Nan answered shortly. She was not going to discuss *that* with any stranger.

"Must be funny, having a stepbrother all of a sudden. Why doesn't he go to school with you?"

At least Nan knew the answer to that. "Because his father went to the Academy, and he wants Chris to go there as long as he came to live here now."

"Are you all going to live here? I thought you were living with your aunt—"

"Chris's aunt," Nan corrected. "I don't know if we're going to live here or not. Mother has to travel—for her writing. She's in Mexico now."

"Is she going to keep on traveling, even if she's married?"

"Martha!" Mrs. Ames did not turn her head, but there was a sharpness in her voice which made Martha redden. She looked away from Nan, stared out the window on her side of the car. Nan guessed that this was not going to make Martha like her any better. Luckily they pulled in to the school parking lot a moment later, and Mrs. Ames got out to go in, with Nan reluctantly following her. The girl kept her eyes fixed on Mrs. Ames's blue-coated back and refused to look about her.

It was almost four when Nan trailed into the apartment-house lobby to face her bugbear the elevator. She felt as if she had been chased all day. Just like a fox in one of those hunting scenes. Her head ached fiercely, and she was doubly hungry, mostly because she had not been able to eat any more at lunch in the cafeteria than she had at breakfast. If only she were headed for the big kitchen at home where Grandma always had waiting a plate of cookies, or bread spread with brown sugar and butter, and a glass of milk.

Nan hesitated before entering the elevator. To get in there all by herself—feeling so shut in—she just could not do it.

"Got yourself some trouble, miss?"

She looked up at Haines and for a moment lost all pride, blurting out the truth. "I don't like getting in there. What if it gets stuck?"

"It won't. Look here." He went in, and she had to follow if she were going to see what he meant. "See this button?" He pointed to a red one. "That's what you have to remember. If you have any trouble, just you push that one. But it's been going five years, this elevator has, and it never got stuck yet."

As reassuring as that might be, Nan was tense until the lights flashed their way from left to right on the number panel, and the door opened on the right hallway. As she pressed the doorbell, Clara answered it.

"Come in, child. Miss Hawes, she's been waiting. Your empty suitcases now—they has to go down into storage. Seeing as how Chris ain't come home yet, you get his, too, and bring 'em out in the hall. Make it quick; I've got to leave early tonight."

Nan went and got her two suitcases and lined them up. She did not want to go into Chris's room, but Clara had said she must. His suitcase was way at the back of the closet. As she pulled it out, something bumped around inside. Chris had left something in there. She'd better take it out. Because after anything went down to the storage places in the basement, it was hard to get it out again. Aunt Elizabeth had already warned her about that.

She snapped open the case. Just an old dirty shirt— No, that was wrapped around something. The shirt dropped from her hand, and Nan looked at— Was it a dollhouse? It could not be—it was too small. There was something strange about the model. She felt as if it were a real building, and she was looking at it through the wrong end of a pair of field glasses, such as Mr. Placer, back home, used for bird watching.

She had lifted it from the suitcase, knowing that Clara wanted her to hurry, when the door flew open and Chris stood there. The eyes behind his glasses were not half-shut now, but rather open and blazing with fury.

"You snoop!" He seemed to come at Nan in one leap, his hands out. His fury was so frightening that Nan stumbled back against the bed. Her hand struck against the post, and the little house fell, to hit hard against the floor.

"I—I didn't snoop!" Nan found her voice as Chris dropped on his knees, reaching for the house. "Clara told me to get your suitcase—to take down to storage. I'm not a snoop, Chris Fitton, so there!"

Anger gave her power to push past him. He did not even look up. Instead he held the model house in one hand, while he picked something else up off the floor. Nan could see now that the bottom of the small building had swung open like an upside-down lid.

"Is it broken?" she asked unhappily.

"No." Chris seemed to have forgotten his anger. "It just opened." So *this* is what was hidden inside.

Nan came back to peer over his shoulder at a tiny oblong lying on the palm of his hand.

"What is it?"

"A sign, the inn sign!" He sounded so excited that Nan felt she dared ask another question. "Is that an inn then?"

"Of course," he replied impatiently. He was holding the very small slip of the wood close to his eyes. "A red deer. No, I remember, in England they call male deer harts—this is a red hart. And I can fix it back right over the door where it belongs."

"Nan"—Aunt Elizabeth sounded impatient—"where's the other suitcase?"

Chris pushed his suitcase across the floor with a hard shove. "Go on," he ordered, "take it out to her!"

36

Nan reluctantly turned and went. So that must be what Chris had bought in the store. But why was he so excited? What was there so special about this Red Hart Inn?

The King's Hunters

Chris lay with his head turned on his pillow so that if he *could* see through the dark, the inn would be visible. He had spent a good hour this evening fixing that tiny sign, so now it swung from a twist of wire over the main door, jutting out the way it would have done if the Red Hart were a real inn. Once he had set the model on the table, after the fall to the floor had somehow opened the bottom and released the sign, that slab of wood at the bottom was as firmly fixed as ever.

"The Red Hart," he whispered. Had there once been a real Red Hart? Most of the models he had made were copies of famous ships or planes which did exist or had once existed. So he was sure that there *had* been a Red Hart.

Why had anyone wanted to make a model of it? And why had the sign which identified it been hidden inside? Why, why? Chris could list a whole column of whys.

All at once he was sleepy, too sleepy to find a new hiding place for the inn. Why he did not want anyone to see it, he could not explain. *She* had—snooping around! Maybe Clara had told her to get his suitcase; he supposed that Clara must have. But—Chris scowled into the dark. *She* had no right—no right to know about the Red Hart, no right at all. His last thought, trailing across the borders of sleep, was resentment.

Chris was aware first of the cold. He squirmed, trying to find warmth, putting his hand out to draw the covers up closer. But what his fingers caught was not the satin-bound edge of the thermal blanket but rather some stiffer and coarser material.

He opened his eyes. The room was no longer dark. There was a dull red glow at floor level against the far wall. And—he sniffed—smells. Such smells as Aunt Elizabeth would never have allowed in her air-freshener–haunted apartment.

Chris sat up, the rough cover falling away from his clothed body. He was not wearing pajamas any longer, but clothes. He sniffed smells of cooking, burning wood, other things which were very pungent but which he could not identify. Then he knew without question that here was the tang of horse, of people who did not bathe too often, of—

His eyes adjusted to the faint radiance of that spot of red. He had been sleeping on the floor, and the fire was nearly out! Master Bowyer would have something to say about such carelessness!

That other Chris Fitton faded completely from his mind. He was Chris Fitton all right, potboy at the Red Hart, lucky to be that out of the charity of Master Bowyer, and not tramping the lanes a-begging his way.

Scuttling quickly to the dying fire, he set about nursing it again into a respectable small blaze. Must be near morning; that sense of time which he had gained when on the tramp told him it would not be long before Sukie came, yawning and complaining down from her garret, to slap around pots and pans.

Chris rubbed his hands together in the warmth of the returning flames. The chill still struck at his back. But at least the heat on his face was a blessing. His nails were broken and rimmed with black; there were calluses on his palms and fingers.

He hunched down in the warmth, grateful for a short time of quiet here.

They had had a late night what with the Master being gone again. Jem, too. Lucky no one had come for shelter. Being potboy was hard enough, but Chris distrusted strange horses, and to help in the stable was an extra burden he did not want. Not that he had any complaints, Chris told himself quickly.

Not many innkeepers would take in a stranger, give him a whole coat to his back, and a way to earn his keep. Master Bowyer—to think about him made Chris feel as warm inside as the fire did without. He tried to count the days back to when he had had no hope at all, before he had tried to hide in the stable at the Red Hart and Jem had routed him out. He was far more used to taking blows and kicks than he was to such kindness as Master Bowyer had offered him. It seemed very far in the past since his father had dropped down a-mowing, his face all drawn to one side, and his arm and leg deadlike. Three days had his father lain so before he died. Then the squire had turned them out of the cottage—him and Bess. Not a penny did they have between them.

Bess, she went to Mistress Fellows at the mill. At least she got something to eat and a roof there. But there was no room for Chris. So he told her he was off to make his own fortune. Fortune? Rather a chance to starve in some wet ditch! Until he came to the Red Hart.

Chris wished he had some way to let Bess know, and to learn how she was faring. But he had come a long way, or so it seemed to him during those miserable days of tramping. The only luck he had was being so small he could hide, so that no constable took him up as a vagabond to be whipped or set in the stocks before being sent on his way.

"Plaguey cold!"

That was Jem come through the door from the cobbled

courtyard. He was blowing on his red hands and stamping his feet just like one of the stalled horses. Now the ostler jerked off the woolen cap he wore, so lank locks of hair fell to the folds of a worn cloak about his shoulders. Chris moved quickly to one side to make room for him as he squatted down on his heels to warm himself in the full force of the fire. He brought with him the strong smell of horse, mixed with an under one of dog.

"Where's that slut, Sukie?" Jem demanded and coughed heavily. "She'd keep her bed round the clock if she could."

"I'm here, gallows-meat. You'd best speak well of your betters," Sukie flounced into the kitchen. Her overskirt was tied up in front above a full petticoat, spotted here and there with evidence of her labors at spit and boiling pot, in spite of the long apron she had tied around her near shapeless waist. Her hair, turned up under a cap, straggled down about her neck in the back. She had a face the color of the dough she punched and pummeled when she was fashioning a pie, her nose a button, her eyes, under scanty brows, seeming near without lashes, a washed blue in color.

"Put light to the candle, you—" She turned on Chris. "Do you think I can do aught in the dark?"

Reluctantly he left the fire just as Sukie kicked at the tangle of blanket on the floor where he had lain. "Get this out of the way. Hell's own breath, you think to trip me, you lack-wit!"

Jem laughed. "In a fine temper this morning, lass? And what made you so? Did you dream ill—"

Chris, hurrying to fold the blanket, caught that glance Sukie shot at the ostler. Her full cheeks reddened as she snatched down a flitch of bacon and set to sawing at it with a long knife.

"Laugh will you!" She dealt fiercely with the bacon. " 'Tis deaf-eared and lack-witted you are, Jem. Dreams, they do tell one things—true things. If I dream ill, there be a good reason to watch ahead."

41

"And you dreamed ill?" he asked.

She had her back to him and did not look around, but she hunched her shoulders as if to set a barrier between them.

"Dreams be chancy things," Jem added after a moment of silence. "Best not depend upon 'em, lass."

Sukie snorted and kept on with her preparations for breakfast. Master Bowyer was not like some innkeepers who had one table for his guests, another for those who served. Chris's mouth watered. In due time he would have a good fistful of bread with a sizzling bit of bacon in its folds, a slab of cheese, and a measure of ale with no grudging.

"This be baking day." She ignored Jem, speaking to Chris as he lighted the thick tallow candle in its stand, bringing it to the table. "You'll get ready the wood for that."

He nodded. The oven was outside, next to the wall of the scullery which he knew very well indeed, that being where he sloshed Sukie's various pans in sand and water until she declared them clean. Untidy as she might be in person, Sukie was remarkably careful of her tools of trade and not one to use last night's grease in a pot to flavor this night's supper.

"We'll have us company today—"

Jem had been almost to the door. Now he swung around quickly. "It's an ill day for travelin'. There's the smell of snow in the air," he stated flatly.

Sukie shrugged. "There be them as no snow can stop."

Chris was caught by her tone; it was almost as if Sukie were uttering a warning. They got a goodly amount of trade that was certain, being as they were on the road out of Rye. And the Red Hart was no bush hole with only tramping people to deal with. Gentry stayed here more often than not. The tale was, as Sukie had many times told Chris, that in the old days once, a King himself had sheltered within these walls. Of course, that had been in the days of the Old Faith when the Abbey monks had run part of the Red Hart as a guesting house.

Master Plumm—he who had bought the place back in King Henry's day, after the monks had all been turned out—he had kept the guesting house and added to it. Thought to set himself up as a squire or the like, had Master Plumm. But he had died with the flux, leaving no heir to follow him. So, in time, it had become an inn.

But Chris, sometimes pressed into aiding with the waiting in the private rooms, marveled at the fine paneling on the walls, the great carved staircase up which Master Bowyer would show the gentry with a dignity as complete as if *he* were a squire and this a manor.

Jem came back to face Sukie across the big table where her hands were busy with familiar tasks. "What have you heard then, woman!"

She faced him eye to eye, for Sukie was tall for a woman and Jem had the small, rather wizened body Chris had somehow come to think of as proper for a stableman.

"The King's Men—them as are called Pursuivants—have been nosin' about over to Hockenly. 'Twas the peddler as brought the word when he were a-hunting me out a reel of thread yesterday. Happen, they'll come ridin' hereabouts, too. There's a-plenty as follows the Old Faith still, mum-jawed as they be about it."

Jem rubbed his chin with his hand. A three-day grayish stubble sprouted there. Jem shaved only of a Saturday as Chris well knew, he doing the fetching of the hot water for that task.

"Hockenly is it? But the Pursuivants have nothing against the squire. He does his churching by the King's law and always has. There's no likely fish for them to be a-nettin' here."

"The peddler would have it they're nosin' out a massing priest," Sukie returned.

Jem laughed. "Not here! What would bring one o' them to us? The squire's no friend to any Papist. They'd do better castin' south. Instow has them what has been fined these twenty years for following old ways!"

"You tell 'em that—when they come then," Sukie retorted. "They'd be right glad to have your word on it, Jem Truck. You being so big a man an' all."

Jem laughed again, but Chris noticed that when he once more turned to go he was frowning. Though what the King's Pursuivants tracking down Papist priests, those known traitors to the country, might mean to Jem, Chris could not understand.

He thought about such hunts as he pulled his sacking cloak tighter about his shoulders and went into the yard to see when Sukie's oven wood would be ready. Poor people did not much trouble their minds with the rights of the matter. First, there had been King Hal who wished himself free of a wife and so said that the church was his. Then later came that daughter of his— Mary—who was as firm in saying that the church was the Pope's, and had men burned to prove it.

After her, Queen Bess. And she the Papists made their plots against, saying she had no right to the throne at all. So then it became law that to be a priest was to be a traitor. Men were killed by that law if they were taken. Now King Jamie, he held by that same law. So his men hunted priests and those who would shelter them. Chris shook his head. What did it matter to him? He was thankful for a full belly and a place before a fire at night.

Nan sat in a rocking coach, which blundered clumsily along the muddy lanes. She no longer watched her uncle. For she felt too nauseated with the lurching to do more than hope that they would stop—somewhere—anywhere—before she disgraced her-

44

self by being violently sick. Uncle Jasper was not one to excuse such weaknesses.

They had risen before daylight, Nan still more than half asleep when her uncle bundled her in. Now there was a gray day outside the coach windows, though nothing else showed but a tangle of tall growing hedge walling in the rough lane on either side. She shivered; day was no warmer than night. Though the bed she had slept in had been curtained against drafts and there was a warming of blankets there about her.

Jasper Knype was a King's Man. He could order people about and be obeyed. Nan saw him now peering through the window of the coach as if trying to pick up some landmark among the matted brush. Above a point of dark beard, his lips were set so tightly it was as if he must seal into himself some knowledge never to be told. His nose was large and sharp at the tip, his eyes never still, ever flitting from side to side as if he was in search of other people's secrets while locked upon his own.

It was his duty to the King, he said, this searching out of traitors. Nan huddled closer in her cloak of dull gray. She was now a part of what he did, even as was Sam Dykes, who drove this coach, and Henry Mockell, who rode beside him, and the three troopers who urged their heavy-footed horses behind, trying to escape the splattering of the near-frozen mud the big wheels tossed back at them.

She had been schooled in her duties. Uncle Jasper was not one to spare the whip when it came to making clear his will. She must do again just what she had done before, three, four times— Now she closed her eyes and thought only that she dared not be sick.

Uncle Jasper prayed when he wanted something. Nan had no wish to ask Uncle Jasper's fearsome God for anything. She was a miserable sinner, that she knew, and Uncle Jasper's God hated sinners. It was very hard to remember what life had been like before Uncle Jasper claimed her. There had been Rose and Ann and Mistress Nevison, peace and quiet and no beatings—no soft quiet voice that went on and on until she could do nothing but what that voice said for her to do. She was Uncle Jasper's blood kin, and that meant that he alone had the right to her. She swiftly learned there was no appeal from his will.

"We are near there, girl."

Nan jerked at the sound of his words, as she might have if he had laid a birch rod across her thin shoulders.

"This is a cunning rogue, and only wit will catch him, the foul traitor!"

Sometimes Nan was not sure whether Uncle Jasper was talking to her or just speaking his own thoughts aloud. But she knew better than to avoid listening. In the past he had caught her sunk in her own misery too much to attend to what he said and she had suffered for that.

"You know what to do, girl. Listen and watch. No one heeds such a creep mouse as you. We shall tell the same tale as at Penedon Manor. I must take you to your aunt and so am burdened with you, even when on the King's business. Is it all firm in your head?"

"Yes—yes, sir." She tried to answer promptly enough so he would not say she was sullen and needed another lesson to stir up her slow wits.

"Well enough. You were the right key to open doors at the manor. See that you do as well here!"

"Yes, sir." She did not want to think of Penedon Manor, of how they had looked at her afterward. She had watched and listened. Because she had obeyed her orders, and no one took threat from a young girl, Uncle Jasper had caught a man—a man who might die—and two other men to lie in prison. She could not tell the right of it. Uncle Jasper said these priests were all from the Devil's own company and that they would send those

47

who listened to them straight into the fiery pit of Hell. Nan was never sure of anything any more, save that she feared Uncle Jasper as much as she did the Devil of whom he was so fond of speaking.

The coach slowed, turned in under the arch of a building, jolted to a stop in the cobbled yard of an inn. Henry Mockell swung down and came to open the door, let down the steps. Her uncle lifted her without ceremony from the corner where she had wedged herself and passed her to Henry, who set her on her unsteady feet facing an open door where a tall man stood watching them.

Nan heard her uncle's voice and the man's, but she was too numb with the cold and her own misery to really listen. It was not until after the tall man had picked her up and brought her within to a small paneled parlor, where there was a fire to warm the air, that she paid full attention.

"This is cruel weather for a little maid to be upon the roads."

She gazed into his face. Those words had been spoken as softly as her uncle might have said them. But his tone was somehow as warm as the fire before her, and his face was open and kindly. He wore no beard, and his cheeks were brown as if he were often out under the sun. The hair, which crept back from his high head in a way which left a graying peak pointed between his dark eyes, lengthened to the level of his plain linen collar; his coat was of a dark russet; his breeches of leather; and there were thick knitted stockings above his square-toed shoes.

He smiled. "I am Peter Bowyer who keeps this inn."

Nan flinched. "I am Nan Mallory, if it please you, sir." He was dressed with the plainness of a countryman, and yet she felt that there was about him the manner of a squire.

"It pleases me very well, Mistress Mallory. Now bide you here where it is warm, and one shall bring you a hot posset to drink and an apple tart. Sukie has taken a batch straight from the oven. You shall find them very good indeed."

He nodded as if they were already old friends, leaving with a quick step as if there was much to see to. Nan fumbled with the throat ties that held her hooded cloak. She did not know where Uncle Jasper was, and for the moment she did not care. But she could not help looking about her now with the eyes Uncle Jasper had trained to serve him.

The room was small, and the walls paneled throughout. Even the door, when it was closed, was covered by panels, so that it could hardly be told from the rest of the wall. There was a large fireplace, though the fire did not fill it, and the stone mantel was carved with a tracing of vine and flat roses.

But there was little furniture—a table pushed against the far wall with a candlestick on it, the bench Master Bowyer had pulled closer to the fire for her to sit on, a couple of stools. It was the walls, however, that would yield any secrets.

Those who held by the Old Faith had hiding places in the walls—places where a man might stand or lie when the King's Men hunted them. Those places were secret, but such secrets could be discovered. And Uncle Jasper had taught her how one worked toward such discoveries. Nan uttered a small sound which was near a whimper. She would have to look—soon.

Chris watched the men tramp into the kitchen. Sukie did not look up from the table where she was setting out the loaves, hot and smelling so good, which she had just brought in from the oven. Twice her fingers jerked, and she nearly tumbled a round of fresh bread onto the sanded floor. Yet she did not glance at the men, and her lower lip was caught between her teeth. Chris felt her fear, though he could not understand it. Surely they had nothing to fear here, they were not sheltering any enemy of the

King. Let this officer and his men clatter through the Red Hart from attic to cellar and leave with empty hands.

He could not understand what story had brought them here at all. This was a quiet village, strung out along the Rye road, the cottages fronting each other across the highway, the church at one end and the Red Hart at the other. Everyone knew that Squire Kenton, up at the Manor, was no lover of the Pope. His own brother had been killed in Spain by a priest's urging.

Master Bowyer had raised no protest when they had tramped in with their officer, that sour-faced man now standing in the doorway, his never-still eyes darting about the room as if he expected the Pope himself to rise up from behind the dresser with its heavy burden of pewterware. To think of this being a traitor's hiding hole was so foolish a thing that Chris had stared open-mouthed when he understood they were serious about this search.

Sukie took up a small tray and loaded on it one of the steaming apple tarts, a small tankard of ale, and a spoon. She snapped her fingers to Chris as if she dared not speak aloud. When he came to her, she moved the light burden toward him.

"The parlor—"

"What's to do, slut?" The officer gave Chris a look hard enough to make him drop his eyes. He had seen such before when he had been afraid of being dragged before some parish constable for a homeless rogue.

"Master—he says it be for the maid." Sukie flashed a scowl at the officer. "Master has a kind heart; more than some—"

For a moment the man looked as if he were not going to allow Chris to pass, his gaze straight on the boy as he pulled at the point of his small beard. Then he motioned him on.

"Take it then, fellow."

Chris was glad to be out of the kitchen. Though there had been unusual activity there to watch—such as one of the men briskly measuring the length of the fireplace on a marked stick and another prodding along the stones. As he passed the small chamber where Master Bowyer kept his accounts, he saw another of the King's Men lounging by the half-open door and caught a glimpse of russet sleeve. Master Bowyer must be within, and they had a guard on the door! Chris longed to trip the fellow as he went, but there was no need, he knew, for such tactics. They would discover soon enough that this was a fruitless hunt and be gone about their business. He saw the guard watching him, but as Chris put hand to the latch of the small parlor door, the man relaxed.

Chris entered. Maid, Sukie had said. But did the King's Men bring with them *women* when they hunted? Or was she some prisoner or witness they kept in guard? Yet there was no man before *this* door—

"Oh!"

Here was only a girl! No bigger than Bess the last time Chris had seen her. She stood by the table, staring at him as if he had frightened her. Her dress was creased and crumpled. She might have been traveling for several days, and it was dingy dark gray, its cuffs and collar of linen grimy.

While she was not only plain but near ugly. Her hair was strained back tight under her cap. What little of it showed was a sandy red, as were her brows and her scanty eyelashes. There were thick freckles across her nose and cheeks. Why, Bess had been far prettier. This girl looked as if she were afraid of her own shadow.

"Something to eat, mistress." Chris set down the tray.

"Thank—thank you." Even her voice was like the shadow of a real one. "It is—it is kind of Master Bowyer—"

Chris swung around, taking a step closer to her. "What do you know of Master Bowyer?" he demanded fiercely.

She shrank a little. "Naught. He—he was kind to me. He said someone would bring me food—"

"What are you doing here?" Chris was oddly heartened by her obvious signs of fear. "Why did you come to trouble Master Bowyer?"

The girl shook her head. "I—I came because Uncle brought me. He—I must go to my aunt; it is in this direction. So I travel with my uncle."

Chris snorted. "You know what he is, this uncle of yours? He takes men to kill them. But why does he come here? Master Bowyer is no priest lover! So who sent him to seek what he is never going to find?"

Nan kept shaking her head. "I—I do not know. He tells me nothing."

She looked at the boy who faced her with only the short space of the table's edge between them. He looked very rough—frightening—in spite of the apron belted about him and his rolled-up sleeves. Who was he? Some inn servant? But why was he asking her all these questions? This was the first time Uncle Jasper's story had been suspect. She was sure that the kind-faced innkeeper had believed it, that she was merely in Uncle Jasper's company because it was necessary that she travel a short distance in his charge. She swallowed. *She* must do as she had elsewhere, begin to ask questions of her own. But always before she had dealt with serving maids who had felt sorry for her and were willing to believe the part she played. In the weeks she had been with Uncle Jasper, she had never met face to face one who was angry and suspicious from their first meeting. Nan made a great effort to summon courage.

"Who are you?" Her voice came out firmly enough to give her more confidence. "Master Bowyer's son?"

He shook his head. "I'm the potboy." He made that answer short and did not say his name. But then he added, "Master

Bowyer is not married; he has no family." Now he came a step closer, watching her so intently that she wanted to retreat again. "Who lied about him?"

"I do not know—" she began. Then he interrupted her hotly, "It is *your* uncle who has come a-hunting here. Who said that the Red Hart shelters Papists?"

Nan could only stare. "He—my uncle—tells me nothing. I do not know why he has come here." That was a lie, one of the many which always lay heavy on her mind. Uncle Jasper said that such were not lies when they were told in the good cause, yet Nan hated to speak them.

She wondered if this potboy guessed she lied, he continued to stare at her so fiercely. What lay between him and his master that he was so ready in Master Bowyer's defense? If they were not kin, and he had said so—

"The master, he is a good man!" He paused as if to dare her to deny that. "He should not be troubled thus."

Abruptly he swung around and left, shutting the door behind him with a decided bang. Nan stood shivering where she was. The good cinnamony smell of the tart on the table only made her stomach feel the worse. Yet she must force herself to choke down at least part of it, so there be no suspicion roused that she was not what Uncle Jasper had said she was—a young maid innocent of all his work, on her way to her aunt.

She reached for the tankard and sipped at the mulled ale. The brew was warm, spicy. For the first time she felt warmth within her. Taking the horn-handled spoon, she broke through the flaky crust of the tart. But she ate with no pleasure, only the need for playing her role here. Let it be done and quickly—Oh, let it be done quickly, so they could be away!

All the time she gulped both ale and food, her eyes sought the wall panels. She knew well what had brought Uncle Jasper here: his belief that Master Bowyer himself was other than he seemed—one of the traitor priests perhaps—and that the Red Hart had a secret which served those who came and went within its walls.

There were those who in the days of Queen Elizabeth had gone from place to place fashioning hiding places for priests, cunningly concealed, but some large enough to hold a man in safety; others to hide only those things that each priest must carry if he was to serve the false services he held. If Master Bowyer was himself a priest, as Uncle Jasper believed, then what she must seek was not a hiding place for a person, but rather one for the vessels of the Mass.

Nan could eat no more. The shadows which lay in the corners of this small parlor were drawing in upon her as if determined to push her out. The girl squeezed her hands to her breast and stared wildly around. It was there somewhere—what she sought, what she must find. She knew that as much as if some voice shouted to her out of the very air.

It had been this way before—twice. Something had sent her directly to a place of secrets. She was afraid, bitterly afraid, of that queer knowledge that slipped slyly into her mind, sent her in the right direction. At least that was one secret she had managed to keep hidden from Uncle Jasper. It was—like witchcraft, this being able to find the hidden. And witches were even more of the Devil than priests. If Uncle Jasper knew— Nan shivered and gave a small moan, the sound of which frightened her even more.

Let her just be able to find what she had to, so that they could go from this place! Let her do it quickly—quickly—!

She closed her eyes and waited, allowing that knowledge to come, not fighting it, in spite of all her hatred of what would possess her. Then, staring straight before her, though she did not really see the room, she went, her fingertips sliding across the panels. It was when she approached the fireplace, on the far side, that she found it. Here—somewhere—

Up and down the panel her fingers went. She had found it. She might not be able to open it, but Uncle Jasper would see to that. Sighing, she wavered back to the bench where her cloak trailed down to the floor.

The fire could not warm her now. As always when that—that knowing came to her—it left her weak and sick—and cold, as if life had been drawn from her. Now she must work to find an explanation to give Uncle Jasper, one which would fit her learning where the secret lay hid so he could never guess how she had discovered it. This time she could not say she had overheard any whispers of man or maid. There was the boy— But she did not believe that Master Bowyer would entrust a potboy with knowledge that might mean his own death. No, this time she was caught without any way of crediting her discovery to something Uncle Jasper would believe.

Nan drew the cloak up about her body. To keep silent would be no way out. She did not trust her own courage; she had none where Uncle Jasper was concerned. He had broken her will in the first days after he had taken her, so she was his servant and could keep nothing from him, except the greatest secret of all—how she was able to learn such matters.

She began to cry, hopelessly, silently, the tears running down her cheeks, she making no attempt to rub them away. Always she had feared that this would happen—some day.

Chris slipped down the hall. The King's Man had called Master Bowyer into one of the upper rooms for questioning. He could hear the rumble of men's voices from above the stairway where the searchers tramped from room to room.

Jem was in the kitchen with Sukie and Bet, one of the maids.

They were under the eye of one of the guards now. But Chris had been in the yard when they were rounding them up. And he knew one of the tricks of this place, the door from the stables into the main hall, a door which could be easily overlooked. Sometimes at night Master Bowyer came and went by that door, and Chris had seen him, saying nothing. For Master Bowyer's business was his own, and no man knowing him could think he went so to do evil. But for these searchers to think the innkeeper a priest! Who had told such a wild tale?

Chris paused by the door of the small parlor. That girl, she said she knew nothing, but he did not believe her. She had been frightened half out of her wits. He was sure he could get more out of her, given the chance. Swiftly he opened the door and whipped around it, shutting it silently behind him.

There was little light here. The inner curtains had been drawn to keep out frosty drafts as well as the daylight. He looked for her first on the bench or by the table—she was gone.

Then a faint scratching drew his attention to the far side of the fireplace. She was standing before the wall, feeling along the edge of one of the panels. Chris moved forward, and his thick shoes scraped on the sanded floor. The girl gave a little cry as she faced about.

"What do you?"

Nan gasped; then she straightened. She saw the scowling face, the fingers balled into fists as if this potboy would willingly pummel her to get his answer. All at once a new idea came to her, so strange a one that she wondered why it should visit her here and now. What if she could find the secret place for Uncle Jasper, but find it empty? If she did not see anything in it, then she could truthfully say that it was as she had located it!

"Listen"—she leaned forward—"what my uncle and his men seek—lies behind here." She tapped the surface of the panel. "If they find it . . . your master will be taken, do you understand?"

"You won't tell them." He advanced upon her.

"I must tell—about the hiding place. But if it is empty—What then?"

For a moment she thought her words had made no impression on him. Was he too thick-witted to understand? Then he turned that straight stare from her face to the wall.

"Can you open it?"

Nan gave a sigh of relief, so she had touched him that far.

"I hope that I may." Now she dared set her back to him, call upon that power she did not understand to serve her. Up and down she ran her fingertips, trying to hold within her control her fear and impatience.

It was as if she touched some spot which was faintly warm. Then another slightly below it. She pressed on these together, and there was movement in the wall.

Straightway she drew back, refusing to look at what she had uncovered. Only so could she tell the truth, and Uncle Jasper could read it so with his skill at winning confessions from the weak.

"I must not look at it," she said hurriedly. "If I do—then he will get that from me. He can always tell if I try to lie. Do you take what is there into safety! But—leave the panel a little open!"

Nan pushed past him, her breath coming in gasps, her head turned away. She heard his movements before she caught up her cloak and hurried out.

Chris looked within the hiding place. There was a bag lying there, and he knew it for the one which Master Bowyer carried on those night travels of his. Chris did not understand all the girl had said, but he was well aware that his master was menaced by what lay here. He pulled the bag from the hidden cupboard and pushed the panel near to.

Where could he set it for safety—? The oven! The oven still

hot enough to roast the joint which Sukie had put in when she took forth the bread! Grasping the bag tight, Chris slipped from the room. The girl was going upstairs toward the murmur of voices. He did not know if she were on her way to betray him or not. But he was still free. Down the hall he darted, slipping through to the stable. There was the coach with a man on guard at the door of the courtyard, but his head was luckily turned away. Chris scuttled past the scullery to open the door of the oven. The odor of roasting meat, the heat struck him in the face. He tossed the bag, to hear it clink against the back wall, behind the joint. Maybe not good enough, but the best he could do—

"What are you doing there!" Chris stiffened.

A hand closed tight on his shoulder. He summoned all the courage he had as he looked up into the face of the guard.

"Seeing to the meat. They keep Sukie in the kitchen, and she can't get to it. This be baking day, see—and the week's joint, Sukie puts it in when the loaves come out."

"More like you're thinking of stealing yourself a cut." The guard laughed. "At your age no boy has ever a full belly. Be glad you didn't get caught by your master."

He clanged the oven door shut with one hand, kept his grip on Chris with the other.

"March"—he pushed him toward the door to the kitchen— "get you in with the rest, and don't let me catch you sneaking out again."

He thrust Chris inside with a word to the other guard about not taking his eyes off the brat. The man grunted sourly and sent Chris across the kitchen with an open-handed slap that made his head ring.

The boy crouched on the floor by the hearth. What if the guard mentioned the oven and that officer with the ever-moving eyes was suspicious? They were not safe yet—they could not be. The girl—what if she talked? In spite of the fire Chris shivered.

Nan stood in the doorway of the room where Uncle Jasper sat on a chair, watching his men sound out paneling, toss covers from a bed so they could prod beneath it. He seemed to sense her coming and turned at once.

"There is a queer thing." She brought out the words shrilly, those words she had tried to fit together in her mind on her way upstairs.

"Yes, my child?" Uncle Jasper's voice with the deceptive softness spurred her to a greater effort.

"In the parlor—there is a piece of the wall sticking out. I pulled at it—"

"Yes!" Uncle Jasper was on his feet at once. "Bring that gallows rogue." He motioned toward Master Bowyer. "Now"—he set a hand around Nan's upper arm in a grip which hurt, but the pain this time cleared her wits—"now, show me this strange wall, girl!"

Back in the parlor, she pointed. The boy had obeyed her order; it could plainly be seen that here was a small door. Uncle Jasper loosed his hold on her and took an eager stride to pull it fully open. There was only an empty space behind. With a cat's swiftness he turned to look at Master Bowyer. But the innkeeper showed only a measure of surprise.

"It seems that this house has its secrets about which even I know nothing," he said in that calm voice of his.

For a moment Uncle Jasper's hate and suspicion made a frightening mask of his face. Then he shrugged. "Let the search continue," he said.

But Nan knew he was sure that this was the right place, that somehow Master Bowyer had beaten him. Deep in her for the first time there was a tiny spring of hope. Uncle Jasper *could* be bested. And not by a man like Master Bowyer. *She* had done it—she and that boy!

If a thing might be done once, perhaps it could be done again.

The spirit he had subdued and thought fully broken was coming to life again within her thin body. In time she might even find her own way of escape; she must sharpen her wits and use every advantage. No one was going to make her free except herself.

Chris watched them drive out of the courtyard at sunset. They had ripped and hunted, and left the inn in vast disorder behind them. But they had not found what they sought. Though Sukie was now a part of it, too. She must have seen the bag, or what remained uncharred of it in the oven, when she at last had gone under escort to clear out the roast. However, no one under this roof would betray the master.

The girl—Chris wondered a little about her. He had seen her again only fleetingly as her uncle had bundled her back into the coach. But there had been something different about her— It did not matter. She was gone; they were all gone.

He held his head high as he went back to the disordered kitchen. Master Bowyer had taken him in from despair and maybe even death in the fields. Now he had had a chance to repay, and he had done so. He was no longer what he had been in his own eyes, but something better.

4 Dream or-?

Nan opened her eyes. Her whole body was stiff and aching. It had been a dream, of course! But she had never in her life known a dream so real, a dream in which you could smell things, taste things, be hot, cold—and very much afraid. Yes, there were dreams which made one afraid. Only that was a different kind of fear, somehow. Remembering that other Nan and Uncle Jasper, she shivered.

There came the low buzz of the small alarm clock Grandma had given her last Christmas. Time to get up. She looked thankfully around the room. At least she was not—there! All she could remember was being put back into that dreadful coach.

Nan glanced down at her hands. Somehow she had expected to see those soiled linen cuffs about her thin wrists, but only her pajama sleeves showed.

Scrambling out of bed, she grabbed for her dressing gown. Better make it to the bathroom before Chris got in there. He was so slow!

Chris—Chris had been a part of her dream, a very important part. He had been at the inn, had taken whatever lay in the hiding place— She stumbled down the hall, still bemused by the vivid memory. Why had Chris been a part of her dream? In the dream he had been a little taller, and his hair had been a lot longer. He had not worn glasses either. The boy had been Chris, however, without question.

And the inn—the Red Hart—they had been *in* the inn! Only how could they have? The model was so small you could hold it with one hand. No one could have been *in* that.

Chris flopped over in bed to reach mechanically for his glasses. He always did that in the morning, even before he got out of bed. Sitting up, he looked at the night table. There was the Red Hart, just as he had seen it before he fell asleep.

What a dream!

He touched fingertips to the roof of the miniature building. How could he have known all those rooms inside? He wished now that he had paid more attention when the hinged bottom was open. Only then all he had cared about was the inn sign. That hung safely in place just where he had put it last night.

"Chris!"—Aunt Elizabeth at his door—"Chris, you must get up—"

"I'm up!" He made that statement true by sliding from between the covers. The inn firmly grasped in one hand, Chris looked for a proper hiding place. He finally decided on the bottom drawer of the desk, placing over the model some sheets of paper. He did not think Clara would come looking in there. Nor that girl Nan—snooping again—

Chris paused. That girl—she had been a part of it. He breathed a little more quickly, recalling how she had opened the hiding place and then gone, leaving him to save Master Bowyer. Even though she had looked different in the dream, she was really the same. But why was she in *his* dream, a part of the story of *his* inn? He slammed down his comb, made a face at the glass.

"Chris"—Aunt Elizabeth warning him again.

"I'm hurrying." He gave his usual answer. And he had better hurry; there was no use putting off facing up to the usual—

breakfast with Aunt Elizabeth timing about every mouthful, going off to the Academy. Too bad that the dream was not real. He would like to live at the Red Hart just as he had last night. Sure it was cold, and the work was hard. But— He sighed and, with his usual deliberation, got ready for a day which seemed to him far more difficult to face.

"Miss Crabbit?" Aunt Elizabeth was saying as Chris came to the breakfast table. "Why, I remember her. She had a younger sister, Margaret, who was in my graduation class at Miss Pierce's. Yes, I am sure—Margaret Crabbit—she teaches French at college now. Martha isn't in your class then."

Nan had not looked at Chris since he sat down. She was afraid if she did she might blurt out the question at the tip of her tongue—what had *he* dreamed last night? Chris was, however, his usual sullenly silent self, which first relieved and then annoyed her.

"Martha's class was full." Nan did not see any reason to explain that to be with Miss Crabbit represented a kind of outer darkness as far as Martha was concerned. Martha had completely ignored her at lunchtime. Nan had had to eat—though she had not eaten much—at a table with complete strangers who talked over and around her as if she did not exist at all. Two were girls from Miss Crabbit's room who spent most of the time groaning over homework, saying that they were going to get their mothers to protest about all the Crab expected them to do.

"Well," Aunt Elizabeth said comfortably, "there are other girls to be friendly with."

Nan made no answering comment. As far as she was concerned everybody in the school was an enemy who eyed her with the same wary dislike Martha had shown. She was already secretly counting the days to spring vacation, and that seemed far too long away.

"Chris will walk with you as far as the Academy." Aunt Elizabeth made that unpleasant suggestion as if it were something decided upon. For the first time Nan glanced in the boy's direction.

His eyes were on his plate, and he said nothing at all. But Nan could feel a wave of dislike spreading across the table. She might have accepted that, found some way to escape—yesterday. Now she lifted her chin a fraction.

So Chris did not want to walk with her. Well and good! What did she care? They might start out together, so Aunt Elizabeth would not make matters worse by absolutely ordering them to do so; then they could separate. Nan guessed that even if this city was a lot larger than Elmsport she could find her way.

"Oh"—Aunt Elizabeth had gone to the window—"snowing again. I'll just call down to Haines. He'll get a taxi. There is no use of you both getting colds by tramping through this."

For the first time Chris raised his head and looked around. "I'm walking," he said calmly. "I've got boots."

He got up and left the room before Aunt Elizabeth could answer. She gave a little laugh which did not sound as if she were really amused. "Well, I suppose it *is* different for a boy. I really don't know how to— But you shall take a taxi, dear!"

Nan was willing enough to agree. She felt that Chris's solution was the best for both of them, but she wished he had not made it first.

Chris pulled on his short coat. His book bag was on the hall chair. Now he drew his cap down over his ears, settled his glasses with a firm push of the nosepiece. Taxi! All it would need to set off Canfield was for him to reach school riding in a taxi with a girl.

He called back a very short good-bye and made it out of the apartment door, half-expecting a hail from Aunt Elizabeth. Luckily the elevator came quickly. In the lobby he passed Haines who was listening at the phone, probably to Aunt Elizabeth ordering the taxi.

The snow was falling thickly, curtains of it driven here and there by the wind. Chris snuggled his chin deeper into his turned-up collar. Big storm for so late in the year. Chris trudged on. His dream memory nibbled at his mind, but now he tried to shut it out. He did not want to think about the Red Hart Inn somehow.

Since the taxi was late, Aunt Elizabeth had to write an excuse. Then Nan had to take it to the office at school. By the time she reached her desk in Miss Crabbit's room, the impatience of those she had dealt with left her feeling as if she had deliberately set out to annoy them in turn.

The day, begun badly, continued worse. As Martha had forewarned, Miss Crabbit certainly upheld the nickname which had been given her. Though Nan realized that she was not being singled out for any sharpness of tongue, which met her own faltering attempts to keep up with the class. Miss Crabbit could "keep discipline." She had an exterior and tone of voice which reduced even the boys in the back to some semblance of order, but she was impatient with those who did not work their best.

Nan, still at sea in a class where many things appeared so different from all she had known, was near giving up in despair of ever getting anything right again. At lunch she made the round of the cafeteria without paying much attention to the food she selected. She had a hamburger and a glass of milk, as well as knife, fork, and spoon which she did not need, clattering together on her tray when she turned to face what was even worse than the Crab's class—a room filled with tables, the smell of food, a roar of voices, and no one to welcome her.

She hesitated by a table, then set her tray down where there were two vacant seats. The three girls at the other end talked shrilly, as if to top the roar about them. Nan, in one quick and guarded glance, recognized them as classmates, though it was difficult, even though their faces were familiar, to put names to them.

The blonde one with the very long hair and the blue pants suit with the red-white-and-blue–striped T-shirt—that was Marve. Even Miss Crabbit called her Marve. With her, wearing jeans and a floppy shirt with Cat Woman printed on it, was a girl with her hair trimmed as short as a boy's used to be. She had a sharp nose—

Nan remembered a nose like that. A ghost of last night's dream troubled her mind. Uncle Jasper—he had had just such a nose—though a much larger one, of course, and his lips were thin in the same way, too.

The third girl was the Karen Long who sat just in front of Nan in class. She always looked oddly—or had the two days Nan had seen her—like a blurred copy of Marve. Her stringy hair was darker, a straight brown, hanging in untidy ragged locks, instead of being sleek the way Marve's was. She also wore a pair of blue pants and a red-white-and-blue shirt, but she was too plump for them to fit as well as Marve's.

To Nan's complete surprise Marve got up, slid her tray with a clatter down the table, coming to perch on the chair next to Nan, her two friends moving down in turn. Marve was smiling.

"You live at the Ramsley, don't you?"

Nan still could not believe the friendliness in Marve's voice was meant for her. There was none of that put-you-in-your-place staring with which Martha had favored her.

"Just for a while." Somehow she found her voice around a bite of hamburger she did not even taste. "I'm staying with Miss Hawes." Not *Aunt* Elizabeth—because she was not—not a real aunt.

"I know. M' mother belongs to the bridge club. She heard all about you."

Nan tensed. Would Marve, for all her appearance of friendliness, now ask questions as Martha had?

"M' mother takes *Travel Magazine.*" Marve planted both elbows just beyond the edge of her tray. "I saw that piece about Taiwan your mother wrote. It must be something to travel around that way. You go with her—when there's vacation?"

Nan shook her head. "I lived with Grandma—until I came here." She wondered if Marve would lose interest in her now.

"I bet she brings you things." Marve was watching her oddly. "I bet you've got some wonderful presents from all those places."

Nan chewed at her hamburger. She need not tell any real lie now. Mother had brought or sent some things. There was a doll from Japan, and a turquoise bracelet, and a dress from London. Only the dress had been too small when it came, and Nan had never worn it. Not that she cared because she had not liked it at all.

"Some," she admitted warily.

"You got them with you?" Marve sounded almost impatient.

"No. When Grandma had to move, we put a lot of things in storage."

For a moment Marve was silent; then she nodded. "I guess you would at that. Too bad. The Crab gives extra credit if you can bring in something from abroad to show."

Nan half expected Marve to shove off again, but she stayed. Karen and the other girl simply watched and said nothing, though the girl with the pointed nose smiled. Not quite a nice smile, Nan decided. She felt uneasy as if waiting for something, she did not know quite what, to happen. She was very sure that Marve had not joined her out of a pure wish to be friendly.

"You know Karen"—Marve pointed—"and this is Pat, Pat Wilcox."

They both bobbed their heads but did not speak.

"We're Three's a Crowd"—she laughed as if inviting Nan to share a joke— "That's what the rest call us. You see," she added as if surprised Nan did not immediately show understanding, "when we all got slammed in the Crab's room this year, we sort of joined forces." Marve tossed her head and smoothed back her hair.

"I live on Richmond Street, and Pat two doors down. Karen is around the corner at the Bellamy. So we're near you. Your brother doesn't come here, does he?"

"My brother? Oh, you mean Chris. No, he goes to the Academy."

"That's right," Marve nodded, "he's your stepbrother, isn't he? He'd be kind of cute if he didn't wear those goggles and look like he always had a stomachache."

Karen tittered, and Pat's smile widened a fraction.

"You're lucky," Marve continued. "The Academy gives a keen dance right after Easter. Most of us haven't a chance of getting an invitation to that."

"I probably haven't either." Nan made certain she was not going to be accepted by Three's a Crowd on false pretenses. "I don't think Chris dances. Anyway we don't know each other very well."

"That's exciting." Marve leaned a little closer. "Must be smooth to just wake up some morning and find you have a big brother and all! Weren't you excited when you heard?"

"Some," Nan admitted dryly.

"I'll bet you were." For the first time Pat spoke. But her tone suggested that any surprise Nan might have felt was for the worse instead of the better.

Nan, however, could not help but warm a little to Marve in spite of her wariness. She already knew that this girl held leadership of the room and to be singled out by her might mean complete acceptance. She felt grateful, even if she did not care too much for either Pat or Karen.

So when Marve insisted that she join them on the walk home from school, she found herself pounding along in the now thick snow. Luckily Aunt Elizabeth had not thought to send the taxi which Nan had half expected.

When they parted under the canopy where Haines sheltered, it was with the assurance from Marve that they would be by in the morning to pick her up—in Marve's father's car.

"He won't mind. One more won't make any difference," she said. "M' mother knows your aunt. So I can fix it. You'll see."

Nan felt so much better she did not even dread the elevator as she crossed the lobby.

Chris tramped over her wet footprints in the lobby before Lind, the super, could get them mopped up. His mind was already racing ahead of his body—to the inn. All day he had managed, with a great deal of willpower, not to think about that very real dream. But now he relaxed his control and began going over it bit by bit in his mind.

If it were only *his* dream! He resented the fact that Nan had played a part in it—an important part. During the day he had had a chance to get into the library on the excuse of a project and had tried to find out what he could about the Papist priests whom the King's Men hunted down. There were some facts which made him shiver, the more so when he remembered Master Bowyer. They killed men they said were traitors in a horrible way then.

But at least his dream had not been *that* bad. Master Bowyer had escaped, because that officer could not find any evidence that Bowyer was secretly a priest. Chris remembered how his dream self had hidden that evidence. He had had a lot of luck, being able to get the bag into the oven that way.

That girl—Nan—he still could not figure out just how she had discovered the hiding place in the parlor. It had been plain she was awfully afraid of the man who was supposed to be her uncle. She had said she could not lie to him, that he would know it. But how *had* she found that cupboard? Had she been told about it and been left to open it? Chris rang the doorbell to the apartment with less than half a mind on what he was doing, being far more wrapped in his dream adventure.

Clara opened the door. "Get off those boots," she commanded before he was even inside. "Your slippers are right over there. And there's cocoa ready in the kitchen."

Chris did not in the least want cocoa in the kitchen; he wanted his own room with the door shut and a chance to look at the inn. But he had learned not to argue with Clara.

Nan was already in the kitchen, a mug of cocoa in her hand, choosing from a plate of chocolate-chip cookies.

"These are store ones," she said as Chris sat down.

He grunted, not aware that she had given him a searching glance.

"Do you know," Nan continued, "what tastes wonderful? An apple tart with cinnamon and sugar—"

Chris's hand had gone out automatically to pick up a cooky. Now he turned swiftly to face her. "You—you *were* there!"

"Yes."

"But it was a dream. *My* dream!" he snapped resentfully.

"Mine, too!" She sounded triumphant enough to make him long to slap her.

Then curiosity and the need to know got the better of his flare of temper. "What do you remember?" he demanded.

She looked around. Clara was getting ready to go as soon as Aunt Elizabeth returned. They were alone. But how long might they be left so? Worrying about that, Nan began to retell her night's experiences as fast as she could.

5 Double Dare

"Why?" Chris said flatly when she had finished.

"What?" Nan had begun when he interrupted, "Why did we both dream that? Did it really happen—once?"

Though the kitchen was warm and the cocoa she had just swallowed hot, Nan shivered. "How could it be?"

"Models," Chris returned as if he were thinking aloud, "are usually copies of real buildings, or ships, or whatever. The Red Hart could be a copy of a real inn."

Nan stared at him over the rim of her mug. "Even if it is a copy," she ventured, "what would make us dream that way? Do you believe it all really did happen—a long time ago?" Again she shivered.

"Maybe. I read up about priests at the library today. King Henry the Eighth declared the Church of England separate from the rule of the Pope, who lived in Rome. He considered all Roman Catholic priests to be traitors because they continued to hold Mass in their own way. Your uncle—he was what they called a Pursuivant, one of the King's Men. They went around hunting Papist priests and the people who helped them. It was a bad time."

"He was *not* my uncle!" Nan flared. "He—he was just someone in a bad dream. So there!"

She set down her mug and would have gotten up from the table, but Chris's hand shot out to close fingers about her wrist hard. "How did you find that place in the wall?" he demanded.

"I—it was a dream—"

"Maybe it was a dream, but how *did* you find it? Did your uncle tell you where it was?"

Nan settled back, for it was plain Chris was not going to let go until he had an answer. "I don't know—it was queer. I could—well, sort of run my hands over the wood and feel that it was there. But I couldn't tell Uncle Jasper that." Her fear in the dream flared up. "Because he would have said that was Devil's knowledge. So—so I had to make up stories about how I found the places—at least, I think I did. But"—now she jerked free of Chris's hold—"I don't want to talk about it—even think about it. It was too real. It scares me!"

"Come on!" Chris moved faster than she had ever seen him. Before she could dodge, he had caught hold of her arm, was urging her toward the kitchen door. Behind his glasses his eyes were fully open, and the shut-in look of his face was gone. She could not fight to free herself, for Clara was coming with her no-nonsense, it's-nearly-time-for-me-to-leave look. And Nan, even in the short time she had lived here, knew better than to argue with that.

Chris propelled her down the hall to his bedroom, pushed her in ahead of him, and shut the door. Curious, Nan stood where she was while he pulled open the bottom drawer of the small desk. Sheets of paper were flung to the floor as he stood up, holding the inn.

Nan retreated hurriedly. "No!" she said loudly. "I won't!"

As clearly as if he had said it aloud, she knew what Chris wanted. He wanted her to hold that—that *thing!* And she would not. She must forget all about it. Frantically Nan groped behind her for the doorknob, got hold of it, and somehow scrambled out

74

into the hall. But she did not feel safe until she was in her own room with the door fast shut behind her. She dropped on the edge of the bed, breathing as if she had been running, determined that if Chris followed her she would scream or something. And she was sure that he did not want anyone else to know about the Red Hart; though how she could be so certain of that, she had no idea at all.

Chris shook his head. Girls! You would think he had tried to make her take hold of a snake! Nan was really scared of the inn. But why? He had never held so perfect a model before. Just because of a dream— He raised the miniature building to eye level. The tiny sign swung a little on the wires he had used to fasten it in the proper place. For just a second he could imagine that he was back in the cobbled yard which lay beyond that high arch, that he was hurrying toward the oven—

No, as detailed as that memory was, he thought, it had been only a dream. Reluctantly he put the model in the drawer and repiled the papers over it. Then he heard Aunt Elizabeth come in, speak to Clara.

It took him only a few seconds to shake out his book bag, have things piled out on the desk as if he had been working. Would Nan tell?

As Chris crouched in his desk chair, twisting his fingers into his hair, staring down at a page he did not see at all, he worried. That was queer what Nan said she had done in the dream—run her fingers over the wall and so learned where the hiding place was. But then weird things were always happening in dreams. He just hoped she would keep her mouth shut.

He continued to wait tensely through dinner and the short time they were helping clean up afterward for Nan to blurt it all out. She did not; she just chattered on about some girls named Marve and Pat and how she would ride to school with them tomorrow, talking so fast that it was as if she were afraid *he* was going to say something, never looking in his direction at all.

Nan waited in the lobby the next morning. Chris had gone on, not even giving her a glance as he slouched out the door into the snow which was now fast turning into a gray slush. She was glad he had not tried to get her alone again, said anything more about the inn. It was only a dream after all. And when she allowed herself to remember some parts and could still be afraid, she tried hard not to.

A horn honked outside, and Haines beckoned to her. She hurried to the street and jumped a ridge of grimy snow to squeeze in beside Marve on the front seat of the car, saying a shy "hello and thank you" to Marve's father behind the wheel.

"Did you get your outline done?" Marve greeted her. "The Crab sure piles it on. Then half the time, when you get it done, she doesn't want it."

"This is library day." Pat had pushed forward in the back seat, so her face was just inches away from Nan's. "I forgot my book. Fact is, I can't find it." She laughed as if this was certainly no calamity. "Anyway, it gets us out of the room—and tomorrow's a day off because of teachers' meeting."

Marve ignored Pat's comments. Instead her hand closed over Nan's with a squeeze. "You have anything planned for tomorrow, Nan?"

Nothing, except what Aunt Elizabeth might think up. Chris would be at school. Suddenly the thought of staying in the apartment with Clara all day, or going shopping with Aunt Elizabeth— No, Nan would not be doing that, because tomorrow Aunt Elizabeth had her day as a volunteer Pink Lady at the hospital.

"No," she returned.

"We have—" Marve's excited voice made Nan glance at her,

76

only to see that the other girl was eyeing her sidewise with a measuring look. "Tell you what, you can come with us."

"But—" That protest came from Karen. She only got out the one word. Pat was gone from just behind Nan; maybe she had shut her up. Nan wondered if Karen did not want her to know Marve's plans. She felt uncomfortable again—the outsider. But Marve gave her hand another squeeze as if to reassure her.

It was not, however, until noon, when they were eating lunch, that Marve explained.

"M' mother says we can go to Lumley's tomorrow," she announced. "She said she'd give me the money for the tearoom there, and we can have lunch."

Pat and Karen were watching Nan with absorbed interest. Pat gave her narrow smile and then a nod.

"They're having the month-end sale," Marve announced. "Did you see their ad this morning? All those neck chains reduced one fourth." She laughed.

Karen smiled. "Yes. And the T-shirts—"

Nan had a queer feeling that all they were saying was a cover for something else. She glanced from one face to another. Something out of the past arose in her mind. No, she was *not* going to think about it—that queer feeling she had had in her dream that if she just looked, looked in some odd way with her mind instead of her eyes, she would find out a secret. That had been a dream, and it had nothing to do with the here and now!

"You can come along if you want," Marve was saying. "M' mother'll phone your aunt about it, if you want her to. Lumley's is great for shopping, especially on sale days."

Pat laughed again, and Karen echoed her. They *did* mean something Nan could not understand; she was sure of it. But she was willing to have a day away from Clara's grumbling and the apartment which never, never, would be home.

"I'll ask," she agreed.

Aunt Elizabeth had no objection to the proposed shopping expedition. And Nan was ready by ten the next morning when Marve, Pat, and Karen called for her. Lumley's was not too far away, about five blocks, and since Aunt Elizabeth had already left for the hospital, she was not there to insist upon their taking a taxi.

Nan had passed Lumley's twice, but both times she had been with Aunt Elizabeth. All she had seen were the display windows and the big front doors. Now she felt a little strange about going in with the girls, but Marve led the way as if such visits were ordinary.

The store aisles were very crowded, and Nan was bumped by ladies who paid little or no attention to anything which was not heaped on tables and counters with big red sale signs over them. She had to hurry fast to keep the girls in sight, and it was only because Marve was wearing a bright scarlet car coat that she did not lose them.

They headed straight for the jewelry department where there were jumbles of chains and pins lying on the counter, other necklaces dangling from tall standing rods. She watched Marve stir around in the mass on the table, pick up a pendant made like a big apple, the same color as her coat, and dangle it from its glittering chain. Pat pushed a finger back and forth, intent on the pins, while Karen stood beside Marve watching the swing of the apple as if enchanted by its brightly shining enamel.

"What do you think?" Marve asked, holding it against her coat and then away again. "With my blue shirt—"

"Super!" breathed Karen. "Just super!"

"How much?" Marve looked up at the clerk who had materialized so suddenly on the other side of the counter that she might have risen directly from the floor.

"Let me see." The pendant was scooped deftly out of Marve's

hand, and the clerk turned over the small dangling ticket fastened to the chain. "Four dollars—this is a sale piece."

"About three dollars too much." Marve laughed and shrugged. "Thank you." She turned away from the jewelry counter.

Nan caught sight of a pin—a cat's head set with twinkly stones. She looked at the price on the card it was fastened to—three ninety-five. More than half of her two-weeks allowance. Too bad—she liked it.

Aware that Pat was brushing past her, she dropped the pin and hurried on. Lumley's, she decided, after they had visited the scarves, the T-shirts, and several other interesting places, was far too expensive. At each stop Marve had hunted out some one object and asked the price—even though Nan was sure she could see it for herself—while Pat stayed off a little, fingering through the things, and Karen hovered by Marve's shoulder with extravagant praise for Marve's taste.

As they turned away from the shirts, Nan began to think that this exercise in nonshopping was a boring way of spending the morning. She was glad when Marve said the tearoom was open for lunch now and they could go up and eat.

Marve asked the hostess for a table in the far corner of the room by a window, and when they had ordered sandwiches and Cokes and the waitress had left, she looked at Pat. "Well?" she asked softly.

Pat grinned her narrow grin and nodded. Nan looked from one to the other puzzled. Marve laughed.

"Show her," she ordered Pat.

Pat glanced around. There was no one near their table. She slid her hand from the wide pocket of her jacket. But she held it well below the surface of the table, so that Nan could see but no one else could notice.

On her cupped palm lay the apple pendant. Nan had only a glimpse, and then Pat's hand was gone into hiding once again.

"But—" Nan could not believe in what she had seen.

Marve laughed again softly, her eyes very bright. "No—it's not the same one. But they had three or four—didn't you see? Pat slipped that one off when I asked about the price of the other."

Nan felt sick inside. "That's—that's stealing," she said in a low voice.

Marve kept smiling. "It's a game," she said. "It's a double dare. One of us picks something and asks about it; then the one who has the dare for the day has to get one like it. I've got the money." She patted her wallet. "If anybody ever catches us, we can pay. But nobody ever has yet."

Pat watched Nan with that sly smile. "She's scared stiff," she announced. "But I don't think she's going to blab any. Look in your left pocket, Nan dear." Her voice was sharp and triumphant.

Nan, startled, felt in her pocket. Her fingers closed about the sharp edges of a card. She pulled it out, to see the cat's-head pin.

"No—I didn't—" She was so frightened she wanted to run away from this room, from Pat, from all of them.

"Who would believe you?" Pat asked. "You were looking at it; the clerk probably noticed you. And I'll bet you don't have enough to pay for it, do you? All right. If they catch you with that on you, what good will it do to say you didn't take it?"

Nan shoved the card back in her pocket. She was cold. This was repeating the nightmare of her dream, the horrible feeling Uncle Jasper had brought upon her. Because everything Pat said was the truth. No matter how much she denied it, who would believe her? She did not understand how Pat had put the pin into her pocket; that it was there was frightening enough.

Marve nodded. "Pat played a trick on you," she said as if it meant nothing at all. "Now you have the right to play one on her—give her a double dare. Don't sit there looking as if the world has come to an end. Kids do it all the time—it's just a game."

"Look out," Karen hissed. "Here comes the waitress."

Nan stared miserably down at the table. The pin seemed to weigh down her pocket. She must get rid of it. But how? She could not possibly go back to the jewelry counter and just hand it over. As Pat said—who would believe her?

"Give her a double dare now." Marve was insistent when the waitress had left their sandwiches and had gone again.

"No." Nan had been hungry, but now all desire to even taste the sandwich was gone. First she had been afraid; now she was getting angry. Uncle Jasper had believed he could frighten and bully her into being his spy. And now these three were trying to make her be a part of their "game." She would think of something; she must!

Pat looked at Marve across the table. "I told you," she said scornfully, "she hasn't the guts to try. Look at her. Another minute and she'll be bawling her head off!"

Nan deliberately reached for her sandwich, made herself take a bite, and chew. Somehow it tasted of apples and cinnamon, though she knew very well it was chicken salad. She had outwitted Uncle Jasper—even though that was only a dream. Now she must outwit Pat and the others.

"I won't tell on you—" she began.

"You're so right!" Pat snapped. "Just try it—"

"But," Nan continued as if she had never been interrupted, "I won't give Pat any dare either."

She laid down the sandwich. She could not eat the food Marve had promised to pay for—it would choke her. And she had an idea of what she was going to do. Before any of the other three could move, she got up.

"Good-bye," she said and walked away, refusing to look back.

When she came to the outer lobby of the tearoom, she went to the girl who had charge of the checkroom.

"Please," Nan summoned up her courage, "where do you leave things you have found?"

"You can turn them in right here."

Nan brought the card with the pin out and laid it on the ledge. "I found this."

"Oh." The girl picked it up. "Must have slipped out of a bag. That happens once in a while. Thank you. We can keep it until someone calls. If you leave your name—"

Nan shook her head. "I don't care—it's just that it doesn't belong to me."

Someone pushed up to leave a filled shopping bag, and Nan slipped by, heading for the nearest elevator. She felt the same relief she had felt in the dream when the boy who was Chris had taken away whatever lay behind the paneling in the Red Hart Inn. In a way she had taken a double dare after all, one that those three had not planned. The pin was returned, and she had not told on them. Maybe she should, but to that she could not push herself. Only she wanted no more of their "games."

Now they might try to make things hard for her, Nan believed. She would have to watch out, especially when Pat was around. That the other girl could have hidden the pin in her pocket without her knowing shook Nan.

She made her way as fast as she could through the sale crowds and did not really breathe freely until she reached the street, fearing that Pat and the rest could still in some way cause her trouble.

As Nan plodded back through the slush, she allowed herself really to recall for the first time every bit of her dream. If she had not faced up to Uncle Jasper—why, maybe she would not have been able to defeat Pat today.

But still the inn scared her. She hoped that Chris would keep it right where it was—hidden in his desk—and she would never have to see it again.

She was evasive when Aunt Elizabeth asked her about her day. Yes, they had gone to Lumley's, and yes, Marve had treated them to lunch. But when Aunt Elizabeth suggested that she repay Marve's treat with a visit to the movies this coming Saturday, Nan said she would have to see—that Marve had ballet lessons, which was true as Marve had spoken of them with pride only yesterday.

When she went to do her homework, Chris was waiting for her in the hall.

"Listen." He caught her arm. "The inn—I had to put it in your room. Aunt Elizabeth says my desk has to be refinished and the man's coming for it tomorrow. I haven't any other place Clara doesn't look into—"

"I don't want it!" Nan replied in a low but fierce voice.

"You've got to keep it!" he returned just as emphatically.

Nan could see there was no arguing with him. Very well, she would keep it, at the bottom of her dresser drawer.

Yet when she had finished the book report for the Crab, Nan could not help but open that same drawer once again and pull aside her neatly folded sweaters to look at it. She was both afraid and fascinated. At last, against her will, she set the model on the bedside table. If it just did not look so real!

She longed to hide it away again. But she discovered she could not. However, later, as she settled in bed, she determinedly turned her head away. Though she knew very well it was there, she was *not* going to look at it again!

The Gentlemen

"Nan!"

At first the voice sounded far away, muffled.

"Nan!"

She opened her eyes and sat up in bed. But this was not her bed. In grayish light the ceiling sloped sharply toward one side where there was a small window nearly at floor level.

"Nan!" A heavy thump sounded on the door which flanked the bed.

She must have overslept. That was Emmy who had called her, and—Nan tumbled out of the covers, gave a gasp as her bare feet hit the icy boards of the floor.

"I'm a-coming," she called back. Grabbing for her first petticoat and wriggling that over her head, she tied it tightly over the smock which served her for both day and night wear. There was a second petticoat, a heavier one, and then her wool dress. She snuggled into that, before she dropped on the edge of the bed to pull on thick stockings she had knitted herself and to thrust her feet into heavy, clumsy shoes.

The water she had left overnight in the basin was ice-rimmed, and her breath was white on the air. She dabbed at her face with a wet end of rag and coiled her braid up to pin under her cap. Now there was just her apron, and she was still tying that as she scrambled down the narrow stairs toward the warmth of the kitchen.

Cook would be snappish, and they had three guests in the bedrooms, storm-stayed. Nan would be needed to haul up those big copper jugs of hot water which made her shoulders ache and to take the lady some hot chocolate later. If only Aunt Prudence was not aware of her tardiness! Could she possibly be that lucky?

" 'Bout time you showed, wench!"

Cook rattled pans as she always did when she was angry. Nan did not even try to excuse herself. Cook would never listen anyway. Emmy pulled a face and shook her head warningly. There was no sign of Aunt Prudence. That was one bit of luck.

Emmy had already poured the water into the jugs from the big kettle. Nan knew what she would expect in return for that helpfulness—Nan's breakfast portion of bacon. Inwardly Nan sighed: Emmy always seemed to get ahead of her one way or another.

"To the Doe and the Unicorn," Cook ordered unnecessarily, just to show that she could give orders.

Nan nodded. The steam arising from the jugs burned her fingers. She took a good grip on the handles and started back up the crooked stair the servants used.

The Red Hart had five chambers for those wishing to spend the night. In the old days these had been shared. Now with gentry it was different. Of course each gentleman's servant slept on a floor pallet, and the lady had her abigail in her quarters.

No matter how carefully Nan went, a little water slopped over the top of the jugs. She would have to come back later and wipe that up. Now she set down each jug before the door with its painted design (of a stiff-looking doe and a prancing unicorn), knocked until she heard an irritated answer from within, before clumping back to the kitchen.

Cook was fussing over a tray of the best china, setting out cup, saucer, and chocolate pot. But she did not fill the pot with brew.

"No need to trouble about this yet," she was assuring herself rather than talking to either girl. "No fine miss opens her eyes before the sun is well up. Don't stand there a-gawking, wench," she turned on Nan. "Mistress will be a-waiting her bread and tea in the little parlor. Mind you cut it fine now—no plowman's hunks for her."

Nan wiped her hands on the edge of her apron and took the white loaf, which was guest fare and which Aunt Prudence shared. She was nervous about this. It was easy to cut a slice too wide or shave it too thin. Either way would bring her a scolding. And she must remember it was *not* Aunt Prudence, but Mistress Simpson now.

Not many women managed an important inn like the Red Hart. Mistress Simpson had inherited it from her father, Sam, and she had made it a good place for stopping. Gentry came when they were on their way to and from Rye.

Nan piled three slices of bread on a plate which matched the chocolate cup in pattern, set out a pat of butter that she had churned and worked two days ago, added a small dish of cherry jam to the tray with the cup and teapot. Mistress would make the tea herself from that kept in the locked caddy in the parlor.

Balancing the tray with all the care she could muster, Nan started down the hall. She could not dream of any fate worse than to drop and break a piece of that china. No matter if she was Mistress's sister's child, she'd have a sore back for that!

Aunt Prudence told her twenty times a day how lucky she was to be at the Red Hart at all—after what had happened at Tylsworth. Nan pressed her lips tightly together and tried to push away memory.

Only it was not easy to do that. She saw again the fire blazing high and heard the shouts of the men as they worked to get the animals out of the barn. Then the house had caught—and now there was nothing left but a celler hole with briers growing up about it to hide its ugliness. Da'—he took cold, bad, on his lungs that night. And before the week was out he had died. Mum—she and Ruth, they went back to Granda'; and the land— John sold that. He said as how he was not going to risk going like Da'.

John had spoken out against Da', and Mum had said she did not want to see him ever again. All because Da' stood for the law and would not help "the Gentlemen" by leaving his horses loose for their use at night.

John said there was no harm in acting against bad laws, laws as made it hard for the poor man. If there were those as worked against those laws—like the Gentlemen, smuggling in what poor people could buy cheap—then they were doing all a good turn.

But Da', he said the law was the law. First he sheltered an Exciseman as was shot and left to die. He had a warning the smuggling Gentlemen had left pinned to his door with a knife. Then Da' said No when they wanted the horses. John said they believed Da' went tale-telling to the King's men. So Tylsworth was burned, and all of them—the Mallorys—except John, were looked upon by those who supported or gained by the smugglers' activities as traitors.

Aunt Prudence, she was Mum's older sister who had never wed. People said as how she was not minded to let any man rule her or the Red Hart when her father left it to her. She took Nan 'cause she said Nan was old enough to make herself useful, but she saw to it that Nan worked her way all right.

Nan knocked at the door and came in, dropping a curtsy after she set the tray on the table. Aunt Prudence looked at the silver watch which hung from her belt.

"You are late. Lateness wastes time, and time wastes money."

Nan knew better than to answer. She had learned that quickly enough after she came here. Now Aunt Prudence was critically inspecting the bread.

"At least, you've learned to cut a slice fairly." She spoke as if she begrudged having to admit that. "Well, be off—You must have plenty of tasks."

Nan curtsied again. "Yes, Mistress."

"Then be about them!"

Nan hurried back to the kitchen. If she did not get there in time, Emmy would have gobbled up more than just her ration of bacon.

"So there was he a-holding a fistful of grease and no pony at all!"

Hearty laughter filled the kitchen. Joshua, the head ostler, stood in front of the fire, the back of his stable-smelling jacket pulled up so he could warm the seat of his leather breeches. Cook, a far more pleasant expression on her face, splashed ale into a tankard for his refreshment, while Emmy sat on a stool and gobbled away from a plate resting on her knees, listening round-eyed.

But when Nan entered, Joshua's laughter came to an abrupt end. He eyed her unpleasantly, though a wide grin still held about his mouth.

"We be talking as how the new Riding Officer got befooled." His grin was malicious. "The Gentlemen have a way of sending their goods through. Take their ponies, they do, and shave down their hair, then grease 'em like Cook here puts grease to her skillet. After that, they gets them a good old mare as knows her way through a dark night and strings out the ponies behind her. No need for any man to lead 'em. And do anyone try to catch 'em—like as how the Excisemen did two nights past—they can't be caught. That Havers, he be always up to the tricks—a smart one, he is!"

That was meant for her, Nan well knew. She refused to look at Joshua. Instead she took up the plate Cook pushed at her. Bread and cheese—Emmy had already helped herself to the bacon. She leaned back against the edge of the dish-burdened dresser and began to eat. What tricks the smugglers played were nothing to her, she told herself. Havers—she had heard plenty about him. Though like as not that wasn't his right name. He could be any man in the village, leaving out the parson and the squire.

. They all thought her father had been a fool, those who did not give him the harder name of traitor and say he took information to the Riding Officer. Anyway now it was none of her concern. If Havers wanted to parade his greased ponies down the village street in broad daylight, let him.

"Ho—the house!"

The call came from without loud and clear, and they could hear the ring of what must be more than one horse's hoofs on the cobbles of the stableyard. Joshua jerked away from the fireplace, surprised. It was early for travelers, and he had thought himself able to spend some time in the kitchen warmth. With a sullen look he made for the outer door.

Emmy had crowded to the window, her plump cheeks filled with the food she chewed as she went. In a moment she turned her head. "It's them!"

"Who's them?" Cook elbowed her swiftly away from her vantage point.

"The Excisemen!" Emmy swallowed. "They do have a hurt man with 'em!"

Cook did not look around, but her order reached Nan. "Nan, you go tell the Mistress. This will be for her deciding."

Nan sped back down the hall, knocked on the door, and was in the parlor before her aunt called permission to come.

Aunt Prudence frowned. "What is this—?"

"Aunt, Mistress"—Nan corrected herself hastily—"there are Excisemen outside, and they have a hurt man with them!"

For a long moment Aunt Prudence neither moved nor spoke.

Then she arose from her seat by the table, no expression at all to be read on her face. She moved past Nan in her decisive way and took the other door, which led directly to the stable yard, stopping only briefly to catch up a cloak from a peg.

The snow had been swept off the cobbles by the stableboy, and stamping and blowing here were three horses, their rough winter coats touched with frost as if they had been long outside. One man still in the saddle supported another, the reins of a led horse held with his own. But the third man stood fronting Joshua, his cloak thrown back a little to show his uniform coat.

"What's this to-do?" Aunt Prudence swept forward, that authority which was always hers making both men look quickly to her now.

"I've a wounded man here, Mistress, who needs shelter and tending. I am Robert Leggitt of the King's service."

Joshua spat. "He's an Exciseman; that's what he is, Mistress." He smirked slyly. "You don't want the likes of them around here."

"Be still!" Aunt Prudence looked from Master Leggitt to the pale-faced man with closed eyes. "I hope I know my duty, sir. Bring him in."

An hour later, Nan stood ladling hot water out of the steaming pot over the fire. She had run hither and thither, bringing salve her aunt made from herbs, carrying pieces of old torn linen to the small back room where belated travelers were sometimes packed away on the ground floor of the inn. Aunt Prudence and Master Leggitt had worked together, first getting out a bullet and then binding up the wound. Aunt Prudence thought their patient would be the better for bleeding, lest his fever rise too high, but admitted that the apothecary was near ten miles away and not like to ride this distance in such weather, for the snow had begun again and the cold was cruel.

"There is no right in it!" Joshua held forth in a low mutter with Cook and Emmy for an audience. "It was Havers as shot this fellow. Do you think he'll take kindly to having one of the King's Riding Officers to nurse and coddle? Mark me, we'll not come well out of this! The Mistress has had her way too long; she thinks she's above any man born. Well, she'll learn different. Right that is, Nan?" He grinned at her. "You could tell her a thing or two 'bout them what sets their will against the Gentlemen."

From somewhere Nan gathered the spirit to speak up. "What would you have her do? Leave a man to die?"

"If he'll bring Havers down on us," Joshua returned, "yes. Do you want the Red Hart to be burnt out like your da's place?"

For the first time Cook shook her head. "That he would not dare, Jos. The wench is right. Mistress is only being Christian, taking in one as is hurt."

"Havers might not see it that way."

"Joshua, Cook—Emmy!" Aunt Prudence came in, her bunch of keys swinging from her waist. "You have your tasks, get to them. Nan, the lady in the Leopard is awake. Do you take her up her chocolate, straightway now."

But before Nan had poured the chocolate into the delicate pot, she saw Aunt Prudence confront Joshua. "Put a saddle on Maggie as soon as you can and send Matt to me."

"Mistress"—the head ostler did not move—"if you be minded to send word—"

"I send word," Aunt Prudence said distinctly, her eyes holding Joshua's in a level gaze, "to the Excise station. Lieutenant Fitton who lies here has a young son visiting him there. It is well that he see the boy and soon. Matt is to ride Maggie and lead the horse Master Leggitt will give him. And there is to be no time lost, do you understand me, Joshua?"

The ostler wet his lips with the tip of his tongue. "Mistress, I would do you no good if I didn't say this. Havers will not take kindly to the sheltering of any Riding Officer—"

"Havers!" Aunt Prudence flushed. "Do not quote that house-burning rogue to me! These men are officers of the King, and as such I give them shelter as all law-abiding people must do. I will have no more arguments, do you understand? Send Matt to me—I shall write a note for him to carry, and he is to make the best time he can. Let him know that."

She turned her back on Joshua and marched out of the kitchen. The man stood for a moment pinching his lower lip between thumb and forefinger, his eyes fixed on the door before him.

Nan could delay no longer. Carefully carrying the tray she made her way up to the door of the Leopard where she scratched on the panels, until she was faced by the stiffness of my lady's maid, who took the tray smartly and bade that hot water be brought directly.

Now she had a busy hour, running back and forth. The two gentlemen guests had come down into the larger parlor and were impatiently waiting breakfast, so that Nan struggled with larger and heavier trays. In spite of the confusion Cook had done well. There were platters of cold ham and beef, sausages sizzling fresh from the pan, fried eggs, fresh bread with cherry jam and butter—tankards of ale.

If these guests knew about the early morning arrival at the Red Hart, they showed no curiosity but ate their way stolidly through what was offered them. Both were middle-aged and of sober dress, their wigs small and neat-tied. Save that one showed a waistcoat of brocade when his coat fell open and they both had a fall of lace at the throat, ruffles at their sleeves, they made less show than Squire Allard of the Manor on market day. When they had done, one went to look out the window and shook his head.

Red Hart Magic

"No good day for the road, Thorpe. And with the young lady—No, I would not advise it. We lie snug enough here."

Nan, clearing away the dishes, saw the other man frown. "I do not like this delay. It is very necessary to make Rye as soon as possible. Girl"—he turned to Nan—"get our coachman here. We'll take Jenkins' word on the matter. He is not reckless and will know well the odds."

"Yes, sir." Burdened with her piled tray, Nan hurried back to the kitchen. "The gentleman wants his coachman."

Cook shrugged. "Then go call him; you have still a tongue in your head. He bedded down in the stable quarters last night. Not what he was used to, that one—turned his nose well up, Josh said."

Nan bundled her apron about her arms like a shawl and braved the cold of the courtyard, slipping into the stable. Joshua swung around at her coming. "What you want?" he demanded.

"The gentleman wants to speak to his coachman."

"I'll give him a holler. You get back in before you freeze stiff, girl."

But Nan sensed it was no care for her comfort which had made the ostler say that. He had never shown anything but a kind of sly contempt for her since her coming to the Red Hart.

She darted back into the warmth of the kitchen. Matt had not been there as usual, mucking out the stable. Neither had she seen Noel, the younger of the two boys whom Joshua both ordered and knocked about. And there had been something about the ostler which made her more uneasy than usual.

But Cook had plenty to do; the table in the parlor must be full cleared and Nan and Emmy share the washing up. Well, she knew she would get the rough side of Cook's tongue if she delayed that.

The coachman tramped through the kitchen, nodding loftily

to Cook who must earlier have fed him, and went on to the forepart of the inn. In a short time he was back. "The master wants hot bricks," he announced.

"They never be going to set out in this?" Cook said in surprise. "Not with the young lady and all?"

"They ain't thinking of being set on by no smugglers neither," the coachman replied. "I told 'em what a boil your mistress is a mixing here, and they want none of it. She is a hen-witted female to set herself up against the like of Havers. My master, he's been a-going to Rye on business these ten years or more. He's heard plenty of tales and not nice ones either. Them as don't make trouble, don't have it dumped back on 'em. So we're off."

Cook stood where she was, watching wordlessly the coach-man's exit. Her face was set.

"Like that is it?" she asked herself. "Jos, he's been spreading the word fast—and how far, I wonder, now? Nan"—she looked from the door which had closed behind the coachman to the girl—"you was out to the stable. Did you see Noel there?"

Her heart beating faster, for she already guessed the meaning behind that question, Nan shook her head.

Cook nodded. "I thought as much. Jos, he never has liked taking orders from the mistress. Not that she hasn't always treated him as fair as her father did. All right, get the bricks to the fire, Emmy, and hot them up good. You, Nan, go tell Mistress—" She hesitated and then added, "Mind you, I have no real thing to say, but tell her that Noel is nowhere in sight. Best be warned, if a warning is needed."

Nan fled down the hall. She felt both cold and shaky. She remembered too much of what it had been like when Da' stood up to the Gentlemen. Was it all going to happen again?

Aunt Prudence was in the small chamber with the wounded

man. Those two who had ridden in with him stood against the wall, watching her lay a wet cloth on his forehead as he muttered and pulled at the covering over him.

"It's fever," she was saying as Nan came in. "Best one of you ride for the apothecary. At least he can tell you what can be done if he will not come himself. What do you want?" she ended more sharply as she sighted Nan.

"Cook sent me. The gentlemen and the lady—they are leaving. Jos told their coachman about"—she waved a hand to the bed—"they think Havers will cause trouble. And—well, Noel wasn't in the stable—'least I did not see him. Cook thinks—"

Aunt Prudence laughed suddenly. "If you have any other ill news, do keep it to yourself now, I beg of you. Yes, given that information, Havers will indeed be down upon us."

"If you have a wagon, Mistress, perhaps we could—" the younger man spoke for the first time.

"If you move him, like as not he will be dead within the hour," Aunt Prudence returned bluntly. "Also do you think you could leave here and that not be known? It depends now on chance—and that is not good.

"The windows—draw and bolt the shutters," she ordered. "We must make do as best we can. It depends on Matt, whether he is my servant or Jos's. Also whether the Lieutenant's son can summon any aid for us. I made it plain in my letter—

"Now"—she waved Nan ahead of her—"I must see to these parting guests who wish themselves well away from other people's troubles."

Once outside the door she dropped one hand on Nan's shoulder, and with her other, searched out a key from those which hung on a hoop at her waist. "Take this"—she slipped the key free—"and go to my father's chamber. Find his fowling piece and his two pistols, also any shot for them you can. Bring them speedily to the parlor."

The room had a musty smell and was very cold, but it was in order, for Aunt Prudence herself cleaned and dusted there once each month. The fowling piece was so heavy Nan had to drag it across the floor; all her experience with fetching and carrying had not prepared her for this weight. She found the pistols, two of them, long and heavy, too, just inside the chest lying on top of her grandfather's cloak. There was a bag of shot and a powder horn; she hurriedly assembled them all but had to make two trips to carry them down to the parlor.

The grind of coach wheels sounded on the cobbles—those bound for Rye were leaving. It was not until tomorrow morning that the stage from Rye would come by. Perhaps Aunt Prudence could send to the Manor. But that would not do much good. The Squire was up to London with his lady, and Nan suspected that none of his men would come to aid at the inn without his orders.

As she leaned the fowling-piece muzzle up against the table, Aunt Prudence came in. Nan handed her the key. "This was all I could find."

"Well enough. Now get your cloak, girl. You and Emmy are to go across to the Hodgins' cottage—"

Nan shook her head. "No."

For a moment she thought Aunt Prudence might box her ears for such open impudence. Then instead, she sighed. "I suppose you feel you have a right. But this is no game we play, Nan. Havers' men are rogues, no matter what is said of Gentlemen." Aunt Prudence's tone made a lie of that title. "I would not have you here when they come."

"I will not go!" Nan summoned up determination. "There must be something I can do. Carry a message to the Manor—"

But Aunt Prudence swiftly gave her the same answer her own

good sense had given earlier. "To what purpose? The Squire is not there, and none of his servants would lift a finger. There is this you *can* do. Get on your cloak, and take up a basket, as if you were sent upon an errand, and go down the road to Malmsey's. Say to Granny that I have sent you for feverfew. By now all in the village—if Jos has done the work I believe he has—know well we have here a wounded man to be tended. If Granny asks you questions, say that the King's dragoons are on their way here to protect him, for he is an officer of some consequence. While you go, watch well for any sign that we are spied upon."

Nan nodded and went. A little more than a half hour later, she was back.

"Well?" Aunt Prudence took the dried herb packet from her basket.

"I did not see anyone. It was as if all have gone from the village. I told Granny about the dragoons. She said, 'Bad cess to them redcoats.' But she winked at me when she said it."

"They'll all take care in the village that they have nothing to do with what happens. Well, I could expect no more. But Havers will not come before nightfall; his kind slink in the darkness. Emmy has gone. You can make yourself useful to Cook now."

The big kitchen seemed full of corner shadows. Cook made a clashing with kettle and pans, but there was a curious emptiness. She shot a look at Nan. "If you had the sense of a newborn calf, wench, you'd take off with Emmy."

Nan's chin came up. "I don't see that you've run," she retorted.

To her surprise, Cook laughed. "I'm not one for running, not with all m' weight. Anyways, I've been with Mistress since I was smaller and thinner 'n you. She and her da' before her were good to me. I don't see as how this is the time to go skittering off and leaving her. Not with this to hand!" She touched finger to the handle of a mighty meat cleaver. "Jos and Noel are gone though. Rats scuttle fast enough. Let 'em. Now you get to work a-chopping them winter apples. I'm not setting away any work, and we've mouths to be fed here still."

They ate in the middle of the gray day. The snow had stopped. But the wind arose, whistling drearily around the eaves of the inn. The Excisemen, who had brought their officer, had barred all the shutters, and Aunt Prudence herself had locked all the doors in the late afternoon. The men had been out to feed the horses, only to report that the animals were gone, the stable empty.

Aunt Prudence did not seem surprised. But she took to looking at the big watch now and then as she walked restlessly through the rooms, when she was not at the bedside of the wounded man. He was sleeping, though Aunt Prudence roused him once to swallow a potion she brewed from her own stock of healing herbs.

Night came early and fast at this time of the year. Nan stole up to the second floor of the inn to peer out the windows as yet uncovered. There was no sign of life in the village, save some smoke being wind-driven as soon as it lifted from the chimneys. She could not even make out any tracks in the snow along the road. Like those in the Red Hart, the villagers were waiting.

"What are you doing here, girl?"

Nan almost cried out. The man had come into the dark from behind her so quietly she had not heard him. Then she saw his face and knew him for Master Leggitt.

"Just looking. There's no one around."

He pushed her away from the window. "They ain't taking chances, them down there. You be the Mallory girl?"

"Yes."

"Then you ought to know how Havers deals"—he stopped short—"There, I don't mean to make you think of that." He sounded as if he were ashamed of his outspokenness.

"You don't—make me think, I mean. Of course I remember," she answered quickly. "Do—do you think it is true—that the dragoons will come to our defense?"

"Maybe."

But he did not sound very confident, Nan thought, with more than the cold of this unheated room sinking into her now. "You think maybe Matt did not go or take the letter?"

"There's one thing I tell you true, girl," he returned. "If young Chris Fitton gets that letter into his hands, there will be action. He's right fond of his da'—there being just the two of them. He's getting schooling, he is—has a mind to make something of himself. But he's been staying with Lieutenant Fitton for nigh a month now, and I ain't never seen two who were so close. Seems like what one thinks, why, the other knows 'fore he says it. Yes, I would say young Chris would be on his way—did he get that letter! There ought to be three, four of our men at the station—and there's the King's dragoons—"

"Look!" Nan pointed past him. But already that shadow she was sure she had seen was gone.

"What did you see?" Leggitt demanded.

"Down there—by that tree. I thought I saw something move."

"There's a deal of wind shaking those bushes. Could be you saw just that. But you tell 'em below that I'm staying here to watch."

Nan hurried down the stairs. She was sure she had not seen any waving branch, rather that someone had slipped from one bit of cover to another.

Delivering her message, she found that Aunt Prudence was seated beside the wounded man, a shielded candle making poor

effort to light the room. She was knitting steadily, much as Nan had seen her sit many times of an evening in her own parlor. But on the table beside the candle lay one of the pistols loaded and cocked as Nan well knew.

Chris Fitton crouched against the bushes and put his hands to his mouth. His fingers were so cold they were stiff, and blowing on the ice-matted wool of his mittens did little good. The inn was a big black bulk in the twilight. He could not see the slightest sign of light. Surely if his father had been as badly hurt as the latter reported they would not have tried to move him!

Ever since he had left the clumping dragoons about a mile back and had ridden on faster ahead, he had known that he must be cautious, as wary as if he were a fox with hounds on his trail. He had left his horse hidden in the brush so that it would be easier to get to the inn unseen. At least Sergeant Johnston knew his father well enough to be willing to turn out his men when the warning came.

He had to get in the inn, though he remembered what he had gleaned in the way of information from the boy who brought the letter. This Havers had half the country so afeared of him that no one would stir a hand to help. At least the woman had taken his father into shelter, and maybe she—

Chris measured the distance between the opening to the courtyard and his present hiding place. He ought to be able to make that easily, if he was surefooted enough not to slip in the snow.

And he did, though he slipped on the cobbles within and went to his knees, scrambling up again quickly. He had the buildings in mind, just the way Matt had told him. To his right now one of those tightly shuttered windows must be that of the room where his father lay. He set his shoulder to the wall and hitched along it. At the second shutter he gave a low whistle on three notes.

There was a pause, and then he whistled again, daring to rise this time to his full height and strike twice on the shutter. The sound was so loud in this very quiet courtyard that he shrank even more against the wall, listening.

All at once over his head there was an answering thump of fist against the other side of the shielded window. Then through that barrier he heard a muffled voice, "Who?"

"Chris Fitton!"

"Get to the stable," he was ordered. "There is a door there."

Chris moved with the best speed he could summon, remembering Matt's directions, seeking the horse-scented darkness of the stable. There was already a crack of light, dim but still to be seen. He headed directly for that, as a door swung a little wider and he caught sight of Leggitt, holding a shielded lantern in one hand and peering out into the straw-strewn gloom.

Moments later Chris stood at the foot of the bed. Though there was a candle set on a nearby table, he could see little of his father's flushed face. But that dark head turning on the pillow and the continual mutter of speech too low to be clearly heard made the boy doubly anxious.

"He—he is very ill?" Chris tried to ask in his normal voice, not to show his fear.

"It is the fever." The tall thin woman with the set face changed the wet cloth on his father's forehead.

Chris clutched hard at one of the bedposts, his voice rising high. "Can't—can't you do something!"

She did not even look at him, her attention was all for the man. "What we can do, we have done."

"There's a doctor in Rye—"

Now she did look at him. "He cannot be moved. Nor do I think that now you could bring the doctor to him either."

Chris remembered. "You mean—because of *them?*" He gestured toward the wall with the shuttered window.

Before she could answer, the door behind him opened, and he looked quickly over his shoulder. A girl stood there, carrying a tray with a small cup and a jar on it. She moved swiftly to the bed, walking as if she did not wish to spill what she carried.

"They have been seen," she said in a low voice. "Master Leggitt wants him." She nodded toward Chris.

"You had better go for now," the woman said. "There is nothing you can do here at present. If he wakes to know you, I shall send for you at once."

Reluctantly Chris went, but the girl pattered after him. "This way"—she beckoned him on as she passed him in the hall.

Chris came blinking into a big kitchen. Master Leggitt sat gnawing at a lump of bread and cheese. He took a long drink of ale from a tankard to help him swallow before he spoke to Chris.

"You say that the dragoons are coming. It may be that they are going to walk into a trap. There is only one road in, and Havers and his gang could lay hidden at any of a dozen places along it. Our men wouldn't have a chance."

"You think they'd dare attack the dragoons?"

"Havers will," the Exciseman said. "He hates Master Leggitt with a black hate—has sworn half a hundred times he'll see him dead to pay for his brother, as the Lieutenant took for hanging. He is no common porter or henchman, look you. The whole of this part of the countryside is afraid of his bullyboys. I think why he has held off rushing us so far is because he wants to get any help sent us into the bargain. To win a victory over dragoons as well as Excisemen will prove that he is as great a man as he thinks he is—make his rule here that more safe. We can't let the dragoons ride in unknowing of the danger."

"There is a way—"

Both of them were startled, for it was the girl who had spoken. For the first time Chris really looked at her. She was thin and tall—rather like the woman who nursed his father—her hair braided up under a plain maid's cap, her dress that of a chambermaid with not even small pretensions toward any fashion. With longish nose and a wide mouth, she was not such as anyone would look at twice. Only her eyes were different. Now they were fully open and looked greenish as might a cat's in the glow of the fire.

"What do you know then?" Master Leggitt demanded.

"There is a side way; it runs through the woods. Men cannot ride it, but they can walk it, leading their horses—"

"If it is known then, Havers will have it watched also."

"But it is not known to any save those who live hereabouts. I do not think he will expect any local person to give the dragoons a guide."

"He would see any venturing forth from the inn." Master Leggitt rested chin on fist, watching her narrowly.

"Perhaps—perhaps not. There is snow, master. If one were dressed in white and dropped from a window to the back, using great caution, there is a chance."

"Dressed in white?" Chris echoed. He understood Master Leggitt's fears. If there was any way out, then they must look for it.

The girl waved a hand. "We have sheets in plenty; they can be made into cloaks."

"And your guide? Your menfolk have made off—"

"Me," she answered simply. "Remember, master, I have a quarrel with this Havers, too. I am Nan Mallory, and near a year agone—"

"Just so." Master Leggitt nodded. "But a young maid—no."

"Yes," returned Nan as if she were bracing herself for some effort. Chris saw that her hands were tightly clasped over the band of her apron.

"I cannot let—"

"You have no choice this night!" Her voice held almost the

same ring of authority Chris had heard from the woman with his father.

"I'll go"—Chris found his own voice—"if she can show me the way. Sergeant Johnston knows my voice; he might not listen to a stranger out of the dark."

"I do not like it."

"We may have no other choice!" Chris returned.

Nan looked from one to the other. "I shall get the sheets," she said.

But she was far from feeling brave as she slashed holes in the sheets so these could serve as cloaks. Somewhat to Nan's own surprise Aunt Prudence had favored her plan, but she had insisted that they venture no farther than the crossroads, circling around toward that from the woods.

"You know the danger in this?" she had asked Nan privately. "Havers and his henchmen—"

"I have seen what they do," Nan found courage to answer. "They may try to burn the Red Hart. And no one in this village will come to help."

"If you will go, then be quick and also careful." Aunt Prudence turned her head to speak to the boy. "Try no heroical attacks; it is enough for both of you to carry the message."

Nan watched the boy. There was little likeness in his face or coloring to the wounded man. He had light hair tied back with a cord, and his skin was brown as if he were much out of doors. He could have been Matt or Noel or any of the stableboys she had seen come and go, save that there was a look about his mouth and a square set to his chin which was different in a way she could not describe.

Now here she was cutting up good sheets while he stood talking to Master Leggitt, who was impressing this and that piece of caution on him.

With one corner of sheet tied over their heads to form hoods, and the rest bundled and looped about them, they slipped through the window where Master Leggitt stood on guard, ready to snap shut the shutter as soon as he saw them safely into the berry bushes beyond.

Nan's heart beat so heavily that she found it hard to breathe. The worst was to expect any moment to hear a cry out of the shadows, maybe even the roar of a pistol. As they reached the poor shelter of the bushes, with the orchard snowbound beyond, she felt weak with relief.

Here she had to take the lead, slipping from one tree to the next; then came the hedge. Beside that, they went to hands and knees, crawling along, halting and flattening themselves in the snow at any sound.

At the break in the hedge, Nan forced her way through, holding branches so these not snap back in Chris's face. She had heard nothing but the small sounds of their own passage and the moan of the wind.

They were in the wood now, along the edge of the Manor land. This was no night for a gamekeeper to be on patrol, and if they could follow to the drive, it would be easy to reach the crossroads. Nan knew that they must hurry. The dragoons had not been too far behind Chris Fitton when he had left them earlier that morning to ride ahead.

Gasping and stumbling, she forged on, holding up the folds of the sheet with one hand, fending off branches with the other. It seemed forever, but at last they came out upon the drive. Nan had no breath left in her for words, so made a gesture toward the left.

Chris took the lead now, she wavering behind. He never looked back to see how she fared but kept at a steady jog while the distance between them lengthened. Then Nan heard the sound of horses. Chris put on an extra burst of speed as she floundered miserably, the snow packing on sheet and skirt until she could hardly keep her feet.

Chris reappeared, behind him a line of dark figures, who, once within the Manor lands, slid from horseback. The dragoons!

"Now then, missy"—one of them, evidently a sergeant, took her firmly by the arm—"if you can just show us this path."

Nan turned around to lead them back. She heard a mutter or two, quickly broken off at a hiss from the man who now helped her along. But she was so weary that the last part of the journey seemed a bad dream. They could see the rise of the inn, a black fortress without any lights; then there was the roar of a musket.

"Well now, that's done it!" said her companion. "All right, boys"—he did not raise his voice very high—"we'll just go in and show this hedge-lurkin' scum what they's got to face. Missy, you stay here! Come on, boys!"

Nan crouched in the drift where she had half fallen as he let go of her. A moment later another hand fastened on her arm jerking her up again.

"I'll get you in!" It was Chris Fitton. "I'm going to see that Havers' men don't get in to m' father—if the Sergeant can't stop 'em!"

He half dragged her back, and they found the shutter which Master Leggitt had closed but not barred. Chris boosted her in the window. Soaked and chilled, Nan collapsed on the floor, hearing shouting and the crack of shots. With a little cry of fear the girl put her hands over her ears, tried to shut out the sounds of battle. Whatever courage had sustained her deserted her now—leaving her very much afraid.

6 "Get Rid of It!"

Nan's eyes were squinted as tightly shut as she could hold them, her hands covering her ears, as she cowered down in a nest of sheets and blankets—

Sheets and blankets?

But she had been on the floor of the old inn, still under the window, just where Chris had pushed her. And the smugglers—!

Nan opened her eyes, blinked at the morning light. For an instant or so she could not believe what she saw. She was not at the inn, but back in her own bed, in Aunt Elizabeth's apartment.

Her hand went out. The inn squatted on her bedside table. It looked dark and ugly. She wanted to sweep the model to the floor, smash it. But somehow she could not complete the swing of hand to do just that.

Nan slipped out of bed on the opposite side, keeping as much room as possible between herself and the Red Hart. All at once she felt cheated. This dream had ended as so many dreams did—in the middle. She wanted to know if the dragoons and the Excisemen had won that battle she had heard in progress. Memory made vivid pictures in her mind: Aunt Prudence sitting by the wounded Lieutenant, the heavy pistol laid out near to hand in the candlelight—the look on Mr. Leggitt's face—Chris — What *had* happened to them all in the end?

And *had* it all happened once, a long time ago?

Nan dressed, glancing now and then at the model warily. As her first flash of fear faded, curiosity grew stronger. What had happened afterward?

Chris lay looking up at the ceiling. He did not try to move yet, though he knew that he was back in his own room, awake. He had been *there* again. But not with Master Bowyer this time—with his father!

He turned his head on the pillow to look at the picture frame on the chest of drawers. *That* was Dad—not that stranger who had lain muttering in fever. Yet even now one face seemed to slide over the other—dream over picture—leaving him still confused. Was he, Chris, sliding over the other Chrises in the same way?

The last moments of that dream—they were all mixed up. He thought he could remember men running away from the front of the inn as there was the heavy roar of pistols and muskets from the lower windows of the building. But—Chris sat up and pounded his fist down on the bed beside him—he did not *know!* Had that other Chris and his father been saved or not? What was real? He had never had such a dream except for the first time at the inn. They were like TV plays—only he was part of them, not just watching the action.

And Nan had been a part of this last dream, too. He remembered how wrapped in sheets they had crept through the woods and down the lane by the Manor. She had used her head, thinking of the sheets, that other Nan, he decided reluctantly.

He had just crawled out of bed when he heard a knock at his door. Not Aunt Elizabeth—she always just called. Chris opened it a crack. Nan stood there, with the inn in her hand. She thrust it toward him.

"Take it!" she said. "I don't want it. I don't want to see it—ever!"

"You said you'd keep it—"

"I never! You just *told* me to! I think you'd be better off if you just smashed the crazy thing. Get rid of it! It's—it's bad."

"How?"

"You know how!" She sounded as if she were working up for a regular fight. "It makes me dream—"

"Then you *were* there—when the smugglers trapped us?"

Her expression changed a fraction when she asked, instead of answered his question, "What happened at the end? I woke up just after you got me in the window. Did the dragoons win?"

Reluctantly Chris shook his head. "I don't know. I remember running down the hall, getting into the room where my father was in bed. The inn woman was there—she had a pistol. And there was a lot of noise and shooting—"

"I wish we did know—how it all came out, I mean," Nan said slowly. "It isn't fair just to know part of it this way."

Chris had taken the inn from her. Now he studied the model. "Maybe we could try again—dreaming, I mean."

Nan whipped her hands behind her back and pulled away as if he might force her to handle the model once more.

"I don't ever want to dream like that again!" she declared. "You'd get rid of it, if you've got any brains."

Then she was gone, hurrying into her own room and shutting the door quickly behind her.

Chris stood staring down at the inn. There were parts of that dream which he did not want to lose. The Chris Fitton who had brought the dragoons, who had come to help his father—that Chris made him somehow proud. He was a different Chris, one he wished he really was.

It was plain Nan was not going to keep the inn for him. He

looked around the room, hunting for a good hiding place. At last he rolled it in a T-shirt and put it at the bottom of his dresser drawer, piling all the rest of his wardrobe on top. That was the best he could do for now.

Then he heard Aunt Elizabeth calling impatiently and huddled on his clothes in the usual scramble.

"I can walk, truly, Aunt Elizabeth." Nan was sitting at the breakfast table. "Most of the girls do. You needn't worry."

"I don't like it," Aunt Elizabeth returned, shoving her coffee mug back and forth and frowning into it. "You aren't used to city traffic and—or are the girls going to stop by for you?"

For some reason Chris noticed Nan's face redden, but Aunt Elizabeth had not looked up. He sensed that Nan found that question a difficult one to answer, and before he had thought out properly the consequence of such an offer, he spoke up, "We go the same way, don't we?"

Nan glanced at him in open surprise.

Now Aunt Elizabeth looked up, as if he had surprised her, too. "Well—that might be good, Chris. But you'll have to hurry if you are going to walk."

Nan said nothing more at all until they had gone down in the elevator, through the lobby, and were out on the pavement.

"Why did you say you'd walk with me?" she demanded bluntly.

Chris shrugged. "She had you in a corner, didn't she?"

Nan glanced away. "Well—yes."

"All right, so I got you out." He added nothing to that but squished along through the dirty slush, looking as sullenly aloof as he always did. Though sometimes, when Nan looked at him, she had the strange feeling that he was another person—two other persons, both of whom she had met in those disturbing, alarming dreams.

Nan dared at last to break the silence between them. "You don't like being here, do you?"

"It's all right." Chris kicked at a lump of gray-coated snow.

"Well, I don't! I wish I was back in Elmsport. I—" She stopped. You could not go on talking to someone who would not look at you, who made it so plain he did not care what you said, or felt.

"Look here," Chris said after a long moment, "we didn't ask for this, either of us. That right? So—well! we have to take it—at least for a while."

Nan seized on that "for a while." Did Chris have some plan which would get him out of Aunt Elizabeth's care? If so, perhaps she could use a similar one.

"What are you planning to do?" she asked.

Now he did look at her, his glasses making him seem to be wearing some kind of a mask. "I don't know what you mean."

"You said 'at least for a while.' "

"*They* have to come back sometime," he muttered.

Nan knew what he meant. "She never stays—"

They did not mention names; there was no need. Nan looked down quickly at the pavement. She was *not* going to let him see what remembering meant to her.

"*He* said that this was the last out-of-the-country job."

Did Chris believe that? That his father would come back for good? Maybe it might be true for him, but for her— There was only one home—Grandma's—and that was gone now.

She did not answer or question his statement. They were very near the Academy. She could see three boys standing by the gate watching them. And she did not like their expressions at all.

"Here's old owl-eyes!" The tallest one moved out a little.

Nan did not see Chris flinch or look any different from the way he always did, but somehow, inside her—just as that feeling had come to the Nan who had searched for the inn secrets—she felt his fear. He—he hated these boys, was afraid of them, too. But he would never let anyone know. She stared defiantly at the trio.

"Got a chick—old owl has," commented another.

They were all grinning in a nasty way, she thought.

"How come you rate a chick?" The tall one blocked their way.

Nan stiffened. Just as she knew Chris's inner fear, so now she read his stubborn refusal to give into it.

"This is my sister, Canfield."

Nan lifted her chin, her own defiance sharpened by his. She stared straight into the grinning face of the leader. He started to laugh and stepped farther out, so that Nan could not get around him.

Then Chris's book bag swung, hitting the other on the arm.

"Sorry"—Chris's voice held to its usual sullen monotone—"I must have slipped. See you later, Nan."

She did not want to go and leave him—not with those three. But she also knew that she must not stay. This was Chris's trouble, and he would have no part of her in it.

"Good-bye." It was not what she wanted to say, but it was all she could think of. And she made herself walk slowly. Maybe if she was still there, they would not gang up on Chris. Because that's what they were going to do.

"Good morning, Canfield, Rocklyn, Fitton—"

She dared to look over one shoulder just as she neared the corner. There was a man standing in the yard, watching the boys. And they were filing past him. Nan drew a breath of relief. Chris might not be free of them, but for now he was safe.

"We're going to have a word with you, man." Canfield crowded against Chris as they started in the door. "You've got an in with the Batman, and you're going to work it—or else!"

He slammed the palm of his hand hard between Chris's

114

shoulders. But if he had thought to send the shorter boy sprawling, he did not succeed. Chris had known enough of Canfield's methods to brace himself.

The bell was ringing for assembly. At least Canfield and his not so merry men—the crowd who followed him all the time—would be in another section. Chris drew a short breath of relief and plodded to his own assigned seat.

So he had an in with the Batman, Chris thought ruefully; that's all they knew about it. Mr. Battersley had a reputation of being tough, but he knew his stuff. And Chris was glad of one thing, that he had managed to keep up in class well enough not to pick up any F's. The Batman did not play favorites; he was impartial about grading. What marks you got in his class you earned, and you did it the hard way.

English Lit was not a class where you goofed off and then passed because you were on some team or your folks came and made a scene in the Head's office. Chris guessed that the Batman could even handle such parents if it came to that.

He was not listening to the droning voice from the front of the room. Rather he was impatient with himself. Why had he ever marched Nan into plain sight? That would give Canfield a lever to get at him, or at least shoot off his mouth a lot. He had been ready to do it before Nan, too. And Chris knew well how nastily Canfield and his gang could talk when they wanted to. At least Nan had not heard any of that.

He was out of morning assembly and nearing English Lit when Canfield stepped in front of him. Chris stopped and stood stolidly still. He had learned long ago that one of his best weapons of defense was to be simply a rock of silence, to stand expressionless and let the other guy wear himself out trying to provoke a fight.

"Owl, you're getting too smart." Canfield grinned at him. "I get some very bad vibes from you. Now we can't have that."

"We sure can't, Canny," shrilled the most outspoken of the backers.

"No, so we're going to let you do the right thing for once, Owl. The Batman is going to run a quiz on Tuesday. He's got it all worked out. So you're going to get a copy by Monday. Then we'll all make A and knock Batman for a goal— Understand?"

When Chris did not reply, Canfield's grin grew wider. He reached out to grab a fistful of Chris's T-shirt, jerking the other toward him.

"I said, 'Understand?' We got gym this afternoon, Owl. I think you need to shape up—we can help you. We want you to be very fit, Owl—fit enough to get that exam sheet. We're your friends, Owl. Aren't we?"

There was a chorus of agreement to that. Then the second bell made a hall-shaking din, and Canfield released Chris, only the promise remained in his eyes. Chris swallowed twice as he settled into his seat.

Canfield meant every word of the threat he implied, even if he had not spelled it out. Either Chris did what was demanded, or there would be an "accident" in gym. And he would be given the rest of the morning to think about that, his imagination going to work on just what form Canfield's answer to his stubbornness might take. He was no superman hero, but— Chris's tongue swept over his lower lip—there was some part of him which would not allow him meekly to do as Canfield ordered. He would have to think. And with that threat hanging over him, thinking came hard.

In the end he used his first study period to visit the library. That was one place where he felt safe; Canfield would not get at him there. He built a barricade of three volumes of the encyclopedia and a dictionary. Behind that, he drew squiggles on a sheet of notebook paper and tried to think clearly.

But all he seemed able to remember was how he and Nan had

crawled through the snow—in the dream. He had been able then to do what he was meant to do. But dreams were not real life—Suddenly somehow the pencil with which he had been doodling began to write out words. This was crazy, but it might work. Of course it would be only temporary, but perhaps if he managed to outwit Canfield and get *him* in enough difficulty, Chris could plan further ahead and stave off disaster entirely.

He had this advantage; the rest of that gang were not in the Batman's first class. They were in the second session because they were in the A lab group. And he was pretty sure that they never did more than the Batman squeezed out of them, either. In fact Canfield big-mouthed how he put it over on every teacher who tried to stuff anything into that solid head of his.

Chris's lips curved into a very faint smile. It would be worth it—it sure would! He'd have to fake something to give him an excuse from gym next week, but that'd be the part he could think of later. Now this was what he was going to do. His ball-point put down a series of sentences. He read it over and crumpled the paper, stuffing it away in his book bag. He would not trust any school wastebasket with this one!

And he was ready for Canfield an hour later with his promise that he would certainly try his best to get the exam.

"You'd better." Canfield flexed his hand, rounded it into a very visible fist. "You're pure prize chicken, Owl. We're not going to part with you."

Chris hoped he was registering the right amount of fear. And he took several rib jabs hard enough to leave bruises, being tripped to fall with force on his face. These were the reminders Canfield and his crowd delivered.

It was three before he got back to the English Lit room. He knew that eyes had watched him go, and he made a business of talking to Mr. Battersley—bringing up the question of a term paper, one he had already decided upon. They must believe that he was laying the foundation for his intended raid.

Though they were nowhere in sight as he came out, Chris was sure all had been reported to Canfield. Now the next step depended upon some hard work with his own portable typewriter in as much secrecy as possible.

He was still laying his plans on his way home when a voice at his shoulder startled him. "Did everything go all right?"

Annoyed, he looked around at Nan. "What're you doing here?" he demanded. "And what do you mean about things being all right?"

She looked a little confused. "It was those boys—" she began hesitatingly. "I thought—"

"You don't have to think anything," retorted Chris roughly. If she was going to come hanging around, believing he could not handle his own life—that would be beyond the limit!

"No, I don't," she fired back. Now she put on speed, marching ahead of him with her head in the air as if he no longer existed at all.

Which was just as he wanted, Chris told himself quickly.

7 Not Guilty

After supper Chris laid out his papers on the table in the kitchen, since his desk had gone to be refinished. He had his Lit book out, and he was concentrating harder than he ever had for real classwork. This must be good enough to pass Canfield's inspection. At least, by paying attention in class and with an excellent memory of the Batman's earlier exam this term, he had a pretty good idea of what might turn up as main questions. The idea was, of course, not to follow the previous exam too closely.

In the end he had an exam figured out. Now all he had to do was type it. Carefully he tore all his practice notes into small pieces, shaking them into the bag for the incinerator. He was so tired his head ached, but he surveyed what he had done with some pride.

Saturday morning he used his typewriter and had to make three copies to be sure that the end result was free of errors. He was so intent on what he was doing that he paid very little attention to Aunt Elizabeth or Nan. Luckily they went shopping, while Clara did not bother him in his room where he installed the typewriter on a chair and sat on the bed to use it.

Carefully he again shredded his final copy. The important part was the carbon, the copy of the exam that Mr. Battersley might well keep in his desk. But how to get it to Canfield? That must be worked out with all the patience and care Chris could summon.

Nan shifted the bag of groceries as she walked across the lobby behind Aunt Elizabeth. She had had to fend off as well as she could two suggestions made by Aunt Elizabeth about entertaining Marve and her pals. That they now ignored her at school was fine as far as she was concerned, though she had been uneasily aware of whispering and the fact that she was again strictly on her own as far as they were concerned. How she longed to get away—away from everything which made up this new life!

"Mail." Aunt Elizabeth set down her bag to use her key on the box in the lobby. There were a lot of letters, but Nan was indifferent until Aunt Elizabeth produced one from Grandma, which Nan had to keep herself from snatching. There was a postcard from Mother—one showing on the picture side a queer stone face—which Nan took with less excitement.

When they were back in the apartment, she carried Grandma's letter to her room and sat down before taking off her coat to tear open the envelope.

Grandma was much better; the warmth was good for her. There was a pleasant group of ladies who met on Monday mornings in the recreation hall to do handicrafts and Grandma's fingers were so much better she could sew again, so she was making Nan one of the new patchwork skirts. She had been asked out for supper twice by her neighbors—

Nan raced through to the end of the second sheet, then went back to the first and read it again. Nothing about wanting to be back home, to have Nan with her again. Only one thing—she read the paragraph slowly, word for word, her desolation mounting:

"I think, dear child, that I have been selfish all these years.

121

Since I made a home for you, your mother missed much of the closeness which should have grown between you. Had I not taken you so completely, she would have seen better the need for this. Perhaps it is well that circumstances forced us into this new life. I am hoping and praying that now you will get to know each other as you should have years ago."

Nan dropped the letter to the floor. The postcard still lay on the bed, that nasty stone face glaring up at her. She poked it with her finger until it flopped over. Mother always typed—well, she had sent about four lines this time.

Striving not to remember Grandma's letter, Nan mumbled half aloud: "Have finished the research. Jeff has two more weeks here; then we'll be seeing both of you. There is a surprise in the making. I think you'll be pleased."

Nan's reaction to that was a sullen *humph*.

She kicked at Grandma's letter, then stooped to pick it up and refold it into its envelope. Grandma was having *fun!* And that piece about Nan getting closer to her mother, she could guess what *that* really meant—that Grandma was tired of having her around! Nan rubbed her eyes fiercely. She was *not* going to cry!

But she would wait a good long time before answering. Grandma could just go on having all her fun. Since she did not really care what was happening to Nan, Nan need not care what was happening to her either.

As for any surprise— She had had surprises enough. And all of them so far had turned out to be the kind one could do without. She shuffled Mother's card against Grandma's letter and stuffed them both in the top drawer of the chest.

Aunt Elizabeth, of course, asked questions. How was Grandma? And Nan reported dutifully that Grandma was much better, thank you, and enjoying her Florida home. And Mother had finished her research. But she said nothing about the

surprise. Chris had a letter, too. He hardly glanced at it while he was eating lunch, and pushed it unopened into his pocket when he excused himself, hurriedly for Chris.

Nan heard the typewriter going in his room. Not fast the way Mother had used it when she came to visit in Elmsport, but slow as if he studied each letter before he pushed the key. It seemed awfully important, whatever it was that he was doing.

Aunt Elizabeth routed him out of his room a half hour later with the news that they were all going to the space exhibit at the Mall. She was determined, Nan thought, to be sure they were entertained—though her own interest in space was not that great.

But it was fun after all to see the pictures and the mock-up of the moon ship, to view the rocks which the astronauts had actually picked up and brought back. The pictures taken of the earth from space were strange. Nan stood before one, gazing at the queer lines which seemed so distorted from those appearing in her textbook. There had been a report a week ago—Gary Evans had given it—about how a very old, old map found in Europe someplace showed the same distortions—and even that Antarctica on it had been pictured free from ice and snow and formed as two islands, which people now knew to be true.

For one moment Nan had a queer, out-of-her-body feeling, as if *she* were floating up in space looking down at the earth. It was a sensation which she dimly realized was close to the feeling she had had in the first dream, when she was sure she could find the hiding place by touching the panels of the inn parlor. What would happen if she could touch one of the moon rocks—not the person she now was but the other Nan who had been able to do such a strange and frightening thing? Would she see—what—? There was not much to see on the moon except rocks standing in tall ridges or lying down.

She walked on. Chris was by the mock-up of the rocket ship. Nan joined him.

"I wonder what it feels like," she said suddenly, "to be shut up in that and 'way off in space." She thought she would not like it at all.

"They travel in space," Chris observed without taking his eyes from the ship. "But what if we could travel in time?"

Nan shivered. Travel in time—like the dreams about the inn? "What are you going to do—with that?"

He made no pretense of not understanding her. "What should I do?"

"I told you. Get rid of it!"

Chris shook his head. "It hasn't hurt us any. Now has it?"

Nan blinked. She tried to answer yes, but she found that she could not. What if she had not had that memory of confounding Uncle Jasper when Pat pulled that trick on her? Perhaps she— No, she honestly did not know now what she might have done. It was that small feeling of triumph the other Nan had had when she outwitted the King's Men which had given her what Grandma would have called "backbone" enough to walk away from Marve and the others who had tried to trap her.

"My father—they're coming back," Chris broke into her own thoughts.

"I know."

Chris continued in his usual dogged fashion. "I always thought that Dad—Dad and I—" He was scowling as he added roughly, "I was a baby. You think of a lot of things when you're little that are never going to add up right, you know that? I wish the part—part about leading the dragoons past the trap had been real—at least *that* Chris did something!"

"It will work out." Nan tried to make her voice sound confident. But she was afraid that she failed, for Chris only hunched a shoulder at her and she realized he had shut her out again.

They had dinner; then Aunt Elizabeth suggested a movie special on TV. This time Chris sat cross-legged on the floor to watch, too. The film was interesting. Nan lost all her doubts and troubles as she let herself be absorbed by the story.

Sunday was church again, and in the afternoon two friends of Aunt Elizabeth's came visiting. Nan excused herself to read in her room, and Chris disappeared even earlier. But she found herself getting out paper to write to Grandma. The most exciting parts of her life—the inn dreams and Marve's invitation —she could not tell. But she tried to make the rest sound as if she were having just as good a time as Grandma, with no regrets for vanished Elmsport. And she did not mention either the postcard from her mother or what Grandma had said about them being closer together.

Monday she walked to school with Chris again, and he was in a hurry, for once. Nor did he talk to her any. There was something wrong—Nan could feel it like a heavy cloud hanging right over the two of them. She looked into the yard of the Academy as Chris, not even saying so long, left her. At least those boys were not in sight.

She faced another day of being by herself. But before she left Miss Crabbit's room in the afternoon, she was called to the desk.

"Ordinarily"—Miss Crabbit always spoke abruptly as if she needed to keep any listeners in line and by now Nan was used to it—"I would not consider this at all. You are behind in three subjects, Nan. However, you have shown a desire to catch up. If you wish, you can obtain the necessary help to do so. Cathy Schmitz will help you—if you can stay an extra half hour in the library each afternoon. You will have to discuss this with your aunt and let me know as soon as possible."

"Yes, Miss Crabbit," Nan answered.

Cathy Schmitz? She was the big girl who sat in the last seat of the second row. At the moment Nan could recall nothing more about her than that. And she did not like the idea of anyone helping her—she had always been an honor student in Elmsport. But she knew that she was not keeping up with the class, and she remembered Martha's warning: if you could not keep up, you got put back a class. She was not going to have that happen if she could help it.

Nan thought about Cathy as she stood before her locker, pulling out her coat. Then she was bumped so hard she was nearly pushed into the half-open locker. She glanced around angrily to see Pat smiling her sly smile, Marve tossing her hair, Karen a little behind her leader.

"What did the old Crab want to tell you?" Marve asked.

"That I wasn't keeping up with the class," Nan said bluntly.

"She'll put you back a grade then." There was satisfaction in Pat's smile.

"What did you do—about that thing?" Karen shot her question as if she must have an answer, but she was not looking at Nan. Rather her eyes darted from side to side as if to make sure that no one else heard her.

Again Nan knew exactly what was meant. "I gave it back." She saw no reason to explain how she had given it back.

"And they took it—without questions?" It was plain Pat did not believe her in the least.

But Marve had been watching her closely, and now she spoke before Nan could answer, "You did, didn't you? But you must have been clever about it—or we would have heard—"

"I didn't tell about you." Nan pulled on her coat.

"It was some kind of a trick," Pat protested.

Marve laughed. "If it was, she's nearly as good as you are, Pat. Maybe you're jealous. Listen here, Nan, we don't want any trouble. If you let us alone, we'll let you alone. We just thought you could take a joke—it's plain you can't." Marve laughed again scornfully. "You're just so square we can count your corners. But if you try to make any trouble"—her eyes were not smiling even if her mouth was—"you'll learn what trouble can be!"

She swung around and walked away, Karen giving a little skip to match step with her, Pat a bit behind.

Nan's hands shook a little as she pulled tight her belt. There had been such menace in Marve's voice that she felt as if the other girl had slapped her in the face. And she still shook as she started the walk home.

It gave her a feeling of relief when she came in sight of the Academy gate and saw before her a hunch-shouldered figure, stalking along the pavement. She could recognize Chris anywhere, and he was alone. Nan hurried her pace to catch up with him.

Chris was only half aware that he was safely out on the street—alone. It had been so easy that he was suspicious. Usually things never worked for him without one hitch or another. But Canfield had taken the carbon, looked down the list of questions, and had accepted it as the real thing. Chris sniffled experimentally. He would have the flu, he decided; just enough to put him out of school for the rest of the week. There was no sense in going in tomorrow when Canfield and the others would discover just what he had done.

A lot could happen in a week, Chris thought wistfully. Perhaps even Dad would think about the letters he had sent saying how he hated the Academy and had decided he would prefer to change to the school where Nan went. It could not be any worse than halls haunted by people like Canfield.

Yes, he would play sick for at least a week. A lot of good

steady sniffling and some coughs— He tried a couple now experimentally and thought they sounded quite promising.

"Chris!"

He half choked on another cough. *Her* again. But he stopped as she came running toward him.

"You're late," he said.

"The Crab kept me after." She would say nothing about Marve and the threat. "I'm behind, coming in the middle of the term. She says I have to have special study.—I'm to tell Aunt Elizabeth."

"Who's going to tutor you?" Chris asked suspiciously. He had no idea of being any part of a cram-Nan action.

"Some girl in my room. I don't know her. But, Chris"—Nan swept from her own concerns to what she remembered from that morning—"is everything all right with you?"

"Got a cold coming"—Chris decided to try out his best croak on her—"probably have to stay out for a while. I get awful colds. You better get away from me."

He widened the space between them as they walked to over two feet and coughed whenever he remembered all the rest of the way back to the apartment.

When they came in, Aunt Elizabeth had just put down the phone. She turned quickly to see them. There was an odd, almost stunned expression on her face.

"Nan, you go on out and get your cocoa. Chris, come here. I want to talk to you."

Reluctantly Nan went on. The conviction that the trouble she had sensed all day had at last hit was strong. But Chris's usual blank expression did not change as he followed his aunt into the living room.

"Chris"—she spoke first—"that was one of your teachers, a Mr. Battersley, on the phone. He had the most—the most unbelievable accusation to make. He said that two of the boys in

129

his second class had a copy of an examination paper which they swear they *bought* from you. They had been caught by another teacher making more copies of it in study hall to pass around.

"Oddly enough only two of the questions were right, ones he does intend to use in an examination tomorrow. But the paper was a typed carbon and does resemble those he uses himself when he makes up his tests. He says these boys have a very straight story that they got it from you, and they each paid you five dollars for it.

"I cannot believe that you would do such a thing, Chris." She was staring at him, Chris thought, as if he had suddenly grown horns and a tail. So he had been too smart after all. Canfield or one of them had been caught, and they had a story all ready to cover that chance.

Chris slid his wallet out of his pocket. He flipped it open before Aunt Elizabeth. "I have two dollars of my allowance," he said stolidly. "You can look if you like."

"I don't need to look, Chris. I know such a story is not true. But Mr. Battersley says I must come in with you tomorrow and get this straightened out."

"My word," Chris said slowly, "against how many of them? You think anyone is going to believe me? Canfield—he—" But there was no use going into all that. Aunt Elizabeth would never understand that Canfield was one of the VIP's as far as the Academy was concerned, and Chris Fitton exactly nothing at all.

"It is the truth, Chris. And you've got to tell it."

"All right, I'm not guilty. And much good it's going to do me!" he flung at her before he bolted back to his own quarters.

His heart was beating fast as he stood behind the door he had just slammed shut. So he was not clever after all, and Canfield had messed him up but good. He didn't see how he was going to get out of this. All the talking in the world was not going to do any good.

Hue and Cry

Chris was afraid that Aunt Elizabeth would keep going on about what had happened. But though she looked at him now and then, a faint frown between her eyes, she said nothing before Nan. So minute by minute Chris relaxed a little. He was still very sure that he had not a single chance of being believed tomorrow, but he had tonight. Though he did go to his room early. Nan had been watching him, too. He tried to shove her out of mind. There was nobody he could depend upon, not even himself.

Unless—

He did not know what very small hope sent him to the drawer, made him bring out the inn. He wished he really could go back in time. Even if it were to the time when the Excisemen and smugglers were fighting. Just at this moment that seemed better than what faced him now.

Slowly he set the Red Hart down on the bedside table. It rested on the letter from Dad, which he had not even opened. He looked down at that—what was the use? There could be nothing in that envelope worth the reading. Reluctantly he got into bed.

Someone was shouting so loudly the noise rang in his ears. And he was no longer in bed. There was cold, with snow, and bushes around where he crouched. Part of the battle with the smugglers? But he had been at the inn then—

He saw a flare of fire shooting up. The inn was afire!

Chris pushed forward. The flames drove away the night shadows. No, that was not the inn he saw across a scrap of field. It was a big barn, and what blazed beside it was a haystack. Men were milling around throwing buckets of water on the flames and then falling back as the fire, as if to spite them, only leaped up higher. There were other noises, and some men were coming out of the barn leading cows. One had a big horse with its head muffled up in a coat.

He got to his feet. Were the smugglers doing this? Why?

"Chris Fitton!"

His name hissed out of the shadows made him half turn. There was another boy standing so that the flickering of the fire showed him a little but not enough for Chris to see his face.

"Who are you?" Suddenly it was very important that he know that.

His only answer was a laugh as the boy slipped back into the shadows. However, it seemed as if some door in his head had opened.

He was Chris Fitton right enough, and his father was landlord of the Red Hart. As to what he was doing here—he knew that, too, now. He had been waiting for Sampson Dykes. And if his father knew about his being with Dykes! Chris drew a deep breath. Right now he should be back in bed at the inn, and the sooner he was there, the better.

Shuffling through the brush, he hurried toward the dim woods path. That was the Manor farm he had seen afire. In this weather they could not get enough water out of the pond to wet it down. To judge by the shouting, half the village was already there.

Chris hesitated. If they kept that up, his father and the ostler

Jack and the stableboys would be coming. He might make the wrong choice going back. But he still padded toward the innyard. Yes, he had been right in his guess; there was the flare of a lantern, men tumbling out of the stable quarters. Chris just managed to join them.

"The Manor farm," someone was yelling. "It's afire!"

He saw his father move swiftly out the door. "Buckets, lads," he called as he came. "And bring horse blankets. We can wet them with snow and beat out the flames—"

Chris snatched up a strong-smelling blanket from within the stable, joining with the force Ira Fitton led back along the woods trail.

They plunged into the fight around the fire, but it was too late to save the barn. Rather they had to fight for the rest of the outbuildings and even the house.

"Set it was!" A man with a smoke-blackened face, who spoke with Henry Nevison's voice, declared hoarsely. "Wickedness it was. Set by some murderin' rogue as would burn us all in our beds!"

The flames were dying. They had at last won the battle. Chris tried not to breathe in the thick smoke.

"It's a mercy, Master, as how we got the horses out. They were so frightened."

"The poor beasts." Nevison commented. "I tell you it was set. And him who had the doing of it, do I lay my two hands on him, he'll wish he'd never been born. Not that it'll do him any good!"

Ira Fitton, nearly as smoke-blackened as the farmer, spoke first. "What makes you think it was set, Henry?"

"How else could it be? The lads know as how there is to be no lanterns ever in there. Plain, I made it to them. And a haystack, it don't burst into fire by itself in the middle of winter! You know well, Ira, there be those who have a spite against the

Squire. He has been hard on men since he sits as Justice. But no man but a devil would turn spite back on poor dumb beasts. If Mick here hadn't got him a bellyache as kept him awake"—the farmer nodded to one of the grimy figures behind him—"we'd have lost all the beasts into the bargain. Murder, I calls it, even if they say as how they is only dumb animals. And how I'm to shelter them," he added, "in this cruel weather now—"

"Bring them to the inn. There's room and enough. We don't get many travelers in winter, Henry."

"What's to do here?"

The man who rode into the crowd, his horse, alarmed by the stink of the burned hay, fighting his control, was older than Chris's father. He had a narrow, long-nosed face with a tight, ill-tempered mouth slashing across it. Squire Mallory. Instinctively Chris drew into the shadows. Master Nevison was sure that the fire had been set, and it was true that the Squire had a dark hate for poachers. He'd sent Sampson's older brother off to be like a slave in Australia for taking a couple of hares when his family was nigh to starving 'cause the Squire had turned them out of their cottage and given it to some gamekeeper he brought from the north.

Had Sampson fired the hay? Chris denied that thought as soon as it came to life in his mind. Sam hated them as hurt animals. He would never have let the farm creatures be caught in any fire. There were other men and boys, too, that had it in for Squire Mallory, that hated him enough to burn up his home farm. Take Jem Catsby, for instance, though Jem had gone away two days ago, saying as how he had nothing here, so he might as well go up to London and see what kind of a fortune he could make. Father had said he was a fool; you found worse in London than you did right here.

Henry Nevison was repeating his accusation and that mean mouth Squire wore twisted a little more. "This is a hanging matter!" he snapped. "And we'll see that someone swings for it."

Chris shivered. Squire meant exactly what he said. He would see as how someone swung for what happened tonight. The boy moved back farther into the shadows. No use letting Squire sight him, not since last week when he had turned white with rage when he caught Miss Nan talking to Chris and asking about the fox pup the boy had raised. To Squire, Chris was not much better than dirt, and no one as his daughter should speak to. Chris had seen even Miss Nan was afraid when Squire sent her home.

"You, Fitton!" Squire pushed his horse near the innkeeper. "What are you and those hangdogs you hire doing here?" He swung his riding crop back and forth in one hand as if he itched to use it, and not on a horse either.

"We came to help." Father was calm. He stared Squire back as straight as Squire eyed him. Squire did not like the fact that the inn was free of his owning, that it belonged to the Fittons and he could not say what they must do.

"And now," Father continued, "since our services are no longer needed, we'll go."

Chris saw the shamed look on Henry Nevison's face. But the farmer dared not speak up; it was as much as his living was worth, seeing as how he was Squire's man.

It was very quiet as Ira Fitton and his people turned their backs on the rest. They did not take the woods trail either, but plodded along the road, mindful not to set foot off that in Squire's seeing.

Jack's voice came out of the dark. "That one will make mischief, Master."

"If he can. Now listen, all of you." There was a stern note in Ira Fitton's voice. "It may be right, as Henry Nevison has said, that the fire was set. But in times when such things are believed, men are apt to seize on the first person and accuse him—guilty or not. You will keep your tongues between your teeth on this matter, and you'll also keep off Mallory land. We'll give him no chance to point a finger in our direction."

"That's well said, Master. The Squire, he takes it unkindly that he ain't master at the Red Hart as he is in the village. He'd like as not point that finger just as you said," Jack agreed; and there was a mutter from the stableboys and the tapman in a chorus of approval.

"So you will give him no chance," Ira Fitton returned. "And you'll do no talking with any in the village. I'll not see any innocent man swing if I can help it, so say nothing because if you do any guessing aloud, it may put someone's neck into danger—guilty or not."

Now he reached out a hand to close firmly about Chris's upper arm in a grip the boy could not throw off even if he tried. There was more his father would say, he guessed uncomfortably, but not before these others. It must have to do with Sam— He stumped through the snow, that grip never releasing him, wondering what he could answer if his father had lighted upon the truth and knew of his slipping out to follow Sam. There was nothing he could offer in defense; he had been warned enough about trespassing on Mallory land and had seen in his meeting with Miss Nan what could come of it. His father had accepted his explanation of that, but he would take very unkindly to any knowledge that Chris had accompanied a suspected poacher.

The men went to bed again in the loft over the stable, but Chris under his father's urging came, not into the friendliness of the kitchen, but beyond into the small room where Ira Fitton kept accounts and dealt out justice to those of his own household. The boy heard the click of a flint and then blinked at the blaze of a candle.

Ira Fitton sat down in his big armchair. His hair was dusted with gray along those sideburns which reached near to the angle of his jaw. And near his right eye was the pucker of scar gained at Waterloo. There was none of the good humor he usually showed in his dealings with Chris shining in his gray eyes now.

"You were out tonight"—he did not make that a question but a statement.

There was no lying to Sergeant Major Fitton, Retired. Chris had never tried. "Yes."

"Where did you go and why?"

"I went to the bushes by the farm hedge." But Chris could not add why he had gone. Father had no use for Sampson. He had said publicly that the whole Dykes family were rogues and the parish would be the better with them out of it.

Ira Fitton broke the silence between them. "It was Sampson, wasn't it? You went with him?"

Chris shook his head. "I didn't see him. He never came."

Sampson could not have set the fire; Chris would swear to that. And if no one knew that he was out that night—

His father leaned forward a little in the chair. "You little fool!" he exploded. "It needs only one man to have seen you sneaking around and tell the Squire— He'd have you sent to jail in Rye before you took a deep breath. And there'll be plenty to curry favor with him by swearing that you're the one. Do you understand me?"

Chris was too shaken to shape any words. He nodded.

"We had better hope that you weren't seen," his father continued.

Suddenly Chris remembered that shadow who had called his name. "Maybe," he croaked, "there was someone."

"Who?" His father shot that at him as he might have shot one of the big pistols he had brought back from the war.

"I don't know." Hurriedly he told of that figure.

His father slapped his open hand down on the table with a noise that made Chris blink. "There's trouble right before us.

Red Hart Magic

I've got to think. As for you—get you up to your room and stay there until I send for you."

Chris scuttled out, fear nosing at his heels as closely as a hound might do.

Nan stood at the window, the thickest and warmest of her shawls about her shoulders. But she was shivering more with excitement than with cold as she watched that distant flare of flames which now died away. Had the farm all burned up?

She had been wakened by a heavy pounding on the door. Liz, who had been in the truckle bed near her, had gone slip-slopping off in her loose slippers, to return with the tidings that it was Dolph Nevison come up with the news that there was a fire at the home farm and there was a need for men to fight it. Nan had pulled out of the big bed and gone to the window to see.

Later her father had pounded by on his horse, heading down the farm lane. The men must have gone the shorter way across the fields. Her father had only been a black shape in the night, but she could imagine his fury.

Only too well did Nan know how much the Mallorys were disliked. Her father might set himself up as Squire, but everyone knew that he had bought the Manor and the lands at a forced sale, because the last owner had broken his neck out hunting and left a widow and two children without a guinea to their purse. And if he had bought his way in here, that did not mean that the villagers, the farmers, the few gentry families hereabouts, accepted him.

She let the curtain fall back into place. Liz had lighted one candle and left it on the chest when she had gone off again into the kitchen to lend a hand in getting hot drinks ready for the men when they returned. Nan longed to slip down there, too, to hear what had really happened. Fear of her father kept her where she was.

He would not have her gossiping with the servants, as he said. She cringed now at the memory of the whipping he had given her after she had gone to see the fox cub that boy at the inn had tamed. Father hated the inn people because he could not rule *them*. Master Fitton held the inn from his father and his grandfather before him. It was one of the tales of the neighborhood which she had heard from Liz.

It all had to do with the smugglers who used to be so important here before their leader Havers was killed—right down in the courtyard of the inn. There had been a Lieutenant Fitton, a wounded officer of the Excisemen, whom Havers had come there to hunt. But the innkeeper was a woman, and she would not give up the wounded man. There had been a regular battle between the smugglers and some dragoons the Exciseman's son had brought in. Afterward the Lieutenant had been judged unfit for duty because of his wound, and he had married the innkeeper and stayed on. So the inn was not part of the village as her own father wished, but remained the Fittons's.

Father had made his money in shipping, and why he had wanted this particular manor, so far from the sea, Nan did not know. But once he had it, he ruled with a heavy hand. Old Aunt Margaret never interfered or spoke up for anyone, and she seemed afraid of Father. Nan had soon learned that you had to obey orders or get his riding whip laid about you. Her shoulders twitched.

She heard a stir below, the bang of a door, the tramp of feet, and the growl of her father's voice, all coming through the crack of the door Liz had left a little open. Dared she go down and see—hear what had happened?

That note in her father's voice was warning enough. He would not take kindly to her appearance. She must hold to her patience and wait until Liz came back and she could question her.

When the maid appeared, she was plainly full of news. " 'Twas set, Squire says," she burst out before she was hardly through the door. " 'Twas a wicked thing to do; they got the poor beasts out, but only just. And didn't Mick feel sick in the night they might have all burned, men and beasts together! Right wicked it was—and Squire says as how the law will make it a hanging matter, too!"

"But who would do such a thing?"

"Well might you ask, miss." Liz looked at her slyly, and Nan knew what the maid was thinking. Her father had more enemies hereabouts than one could total up on the fingers of both hands.

She flushed. It was horrible to be hated, to think someone was so mad as to threaten the lives of men and animals by cruel fire just because he hated so blackly.

"The Squire, he has offered ten guineas—he said it to all who were there—for the name of him as did it. And ten guineas— that is a mighty sum, miss. There'll be men as will come with news hoping to lay hand on that."

"But if no one was seen," Nan began.

"Miss, it was a dark night. Anyone can swear he saw something, and who can say he be right or wrong?"

Nan drew a deep breath. She understood Liz's meaning. If anyone in the village had a spite for another, this would be the time to work that off and get a small fortune, or what would seem a small fortune, in return.

"There would have to be proof," she said with a confidence she did not feel. She knew her father's hard angers. Would he ask for much in the way of proof? And any man desperate or vile enough to betray another would make his story as strong as possible.

"I know who Squire wants." Liz shot another of those sly, unpleasant glances at her. "Master Fitton, he came with his men to help put out the fire at the farm. Squire ordered him away."

Nan sat down on the edge of the bed. She felt very cold inside. Yes, above all, her father would relish hanging such a crime on someone connected with the inn. She did not know the law, but perhaps if her father could prove that, he might in turn somehow get the inn itself.

"That is only suspicion, Liz," she returned as stoutly as she could. "No one must be named without proof. You know that Master Fitton would no more burn out a neighbor than he would set fire to his own place."

"Maybe not him, miss. But he ain't the only man—or boy—at the Red Hart."

Nan got back into bed. The sheets were very chilly about her. She knew what Liz was suggesting. But that was outright folly! Chris Fitton would not set fire to the home farm, just because her father had once ordered him off Manor land and tried to lash him. Chris had dodged that blow—his face had gone very white under the tan, and his eyes had seemed to glitter. He had been wild with anger then, Nan knew that, even if he had said nothing, simply turned and stalked away.

Remembering the whole scene now, she thought that his silent withdrawal had fed her father's rage even more. But she must not say anything which might point up Liz's suggestion. Of course, no matter how much her father might wish to find him guilty, Chris Fitton was not.

But she could not go back to sleep, even though she lay still and breathed evenly, hoping Liz would be fooled. Instead she tried to think of what her father might do. Would he really bribe someone to swear it was Chris or someone else from the inn? If so, was there anything she could do? Over and over again, until her head began to ache, her thoughts followed the same pattern.

Chris pulled off his clothing and rolled into bed. With no hot brick at the foot, it was beastly cold. But worse than the icy sheets around his shivering body was what his father had pointed out and his own memory of that figure who had hailed him from the dark. He tried vainly to remember the voice, and so put a name to the lurker. But he could not. The fact that someone *knew* he had been in the bushes watching the fire remained a threat he would have to live with—

He dozed twice that night, awaking each time with a start of terror from a nightmare. And he was only too happy to have Peter, the potboy, knock on his door in the first light to say his father wanted him. Chris, after he had dressed, splashed icy water on his face, pulled a comb raggedly through his hair, and clattered down the back stairs.

The warmth and the food smells in the kitchen were comforting, but he had to leave those, go on to the room where he had fronted Sergeant Major Fitton the night before. At his father's answer to his knock Chris braced himself to enter.

There was a paper lying on the table. Even upside down, Chris could read the bold outline of the top line of three words: HUE AND CRY. This was the sheet that the Bow Street magistrates sent out to all inns and tollgates in the country, bearing a list of crimes and descriptions of wanted men. His father always posted it in the taproom and read the facts aloud to all those servants who could not spell them out or to villagers who were ignorant of their letters.

Ira Fitton still wore a crumpled shirt with an ash streak across one sleeve, and he looked very tired. He had another paper folded up and sealed with the dark wax he kept for special occasions. With the tip of the quill pen he held, he pointed Chris to one of the stools.

"The mail will be through in a half hour if they are making regular time. I shall give this to Worcester, who owes me a favor. With ordinary luck it will reach London by tomorrow afternoon. Worcester will see it gets to Bow Street, to Harry Hawkins—"

Harry Hawkins—Father had served with him in the Peninsula under the Duke and later they had been together at Waterloo. Afterward, Harry had gone into the Bow Street runners, was one of those thief-takers who were noted for good service.

"I may be crying to arms when there is no attack," Ira Fitton continued. "But given Mallory's temperament and the fact that you were on his land last night, and apparently seen, I think it wise to take my own steps for your protection. Private people can hire the runners when it is a criminal matter. I am asking Harry down to have a look into this. We must hope that he is not otherwise busy and will come."

"You think—" Chris glanced from his father's frowning face to his own dirty hands, still carrying the marks of last night's struggle to beat out the racing flames.

"I think that you have been a fool and that you may be in bad trouble. News came with Tomkins this morning—he made sure I would hear it, so I know that suspicion is already pointed this way—Mallory has offered ten guineas for information leading to the arrest of the one who fired the rick and so destroyed the barn."

Chris swallowed. Ten guineas—that was a fortune! To anyone in the village, it would be a temptation.

"Now"—his father leaned forward a little—"suppose you tell me more about this shadow who called you by name."

"I have been trying most of the night to remember. It was a boy, I am sure. But I did not see his face."

"Sampson Dykes?"

Chris shook his head. "No, I know Sampson. That wasn't his voice."

"Have you had dealings with any of the village boys who might want to wish you harm?"

Again Chris shook his head. He did not go around looking for fights. There were some, he knew, who envied him living in the inn, even the fact that he went to Mr. Preston, the Vicar, twice a week for schooling. But no one had ever shown him active ill will.

"It can well be," his father continued, "that he whom you saw was the actual one who did the firing. As for trying to find one of those hereabouts who hates the Squire more than another, that is going to be a lengthy task. It is more likely that someone will give in a name, either for the money or to save his own neck. And the Squire, being a Justice, can then pronounce his own sentence forthwith."

Chris clasped his hands together more tightly so that his father would not see how they shook. He could well believe it would all happen just as his father said and that he might well be the one named.

"For the moment"—his father arose, the folded and sealed letter in his hand—"we shall do nothing. You will not talk of this matter, nor of that boy, to anyone. You will act as you always do, nor will you answer any questions. Do you understand?"

Chris agreed in a low voice.

Nan pushed her needle through the cloth stretched on the embroidery frame. At the moment she had no governess, so there were no lessons in painting or polite manners or the other things a "lady" must learn. She liked reading, but the books left in the big library, after her father had bought both the house and most of its furnishings, were not very interesting. Many were in Latin, or were volumes of sermons as dry as the dust which lay upon them. She was bored through the long days with just needlework and Aunt Margaret's thin voice, which always sounded near a whine, going on and on about family connections who were dead long before Nan was born.

Aunt Margaret was one of Mother's family, and really she was Nan's great-aunt—a shriveled-up little wisp of a woman who now had only the importance of her own birth to give her any pride. She had early striven to impress upon Nan that her mother was a Ruthven and had given up much to marry a mere Mallory, wealthy though he might be. Nevertheless, as Nan had noted, Aunt Margaret was quick to "yes" her father whenever chance threw them together; which was not too often, since Squire Mallory resented that he did not have a son and made it very clear that Nan was not satisfactory as a substitute.

"Such a pother." Aunt Margaret was sorting embroidery silks, holding one skein against another very close to her eyes. "Depend upon it, the criminal will be speeedily found. Any of these villagers will snatch at gold—"

"What," asked Nan, "if someone says the wrong name then just to get the money Father offered?"

Aunt Margaret sniffed. "It is none of your affair, miss, what is done. It was a murderous thing, for men were asleep there and beasts. This blue is a sad match. I should not have sent Mary to buy it; that girl has no true sense of color at all."

Nan took three stitches. She had become tolerably good at this work and admitted that Aunt Margaret, for all her stupid stories and talkativeness, was a good teacher. They now had ahead of them the project of recovering all the seats of the small chairs in the parlor. Nan sighed to herself, just thinking about what that would mean in years of work.

"Your father"—Aunt Margaret had set the offending skein of blue to one side—"has sent for Hal Chickett's hound. They will cast around for a trail."

"I don't see how they can. Near everyone from the village was there," Nan pointed out, "so how can the dog sniff out the one who was guilty from all the rest?"

"Your father seems to have some information he has not

spread abroad. Now this rose is good for shading, but the other is too faint a color; it will look sun-streaked before it really is. Mind how you stitch, girl." She snapped her thimble-tipped finger down on the edge of the frame sharply. "This is too fine a stuff to have to pick out ill-set lines!"

"Yes, Aunt Margaret." Nan made herself answer that meekly and sweetly. She longed to know what made her father think he could sort out one trail from all those around the farm. And if so, be sure that trail was the right one?

The day wore on dully. They stitched; they had a small lunch in the morning room. Then Aunt Margaret retired to nap, and Nan wandered into the library to hunt for a book. It was a gray day, and the shadows were almost as thick as at evening. Outside the window sounded the soft hiss of falling snow. Nan watched it. That would certainly spoil her father's plan of using the hound. And she found she was glad.

No, Nan told herself in horror, it was not that she wanted the wicked person to escape. But her trust in her father's judgment was small; she was sure he would be only too pleased to fasten the crime on someone whom he already disliked, if he had only a fraction of evidence to guide him.

She crept behind one of the long red brocade curtains, so sun-faded and full of ancient dust that even the vigorous actions of the maids Aunt Margaret spurred on could never clean them completely. The wall here was part of the oldest section of the house and very thick, so that the window was in a recess and there was a broad seat for an inner sill. Nan knelt on it to watch the snow coming down, covering the tracks on the drive without. It was cold, but she had brought her woolen shawl, which she drew more closely about her.

A sound from the room startled her. She did not move when she heard her father's voice raised in that tight tone he used when greatly angered.

"In here, you rogue! And do not think to deceive me. I know very well your mangy stock and that your brother has uttered threats against me. Had I proof of his ill-doing, he would be wearing chains in Rye jail long since. And there would be no mercy to send *him* overseas, either."

Nan squirmed around on the window seat. She inspected the length of the curtain folds before her and sighted what she had hoped might be there—a slit where the old cloth had given away and Aunt Margaret had not yet darned a mend. Using her fingers very carefully, she spread that slit so she could see a portion of the room.

Her father stood on the hearth, still wearing his topcoat and hat. One hand swung his whip, so that the lash caught against one of the fire irons with a menacing and threatening sound.

Before him cowered a ragged boy, a piece of sacking cobbled around him for a coat. His hair stood out above his head in a matted thatch, but Nan could not see his face clearly, only his chilblained hands, near blue with cold, and his feet wrapped in sacking from the top of which sprouted wisps of the straw he had used to stuff about his feet.

"Now"—her father leaned forward, his face sharply eager, as if he were on the brink of learning something that would please him greatly—"now, tell the truth, fellow!"

"It be the truth, Squire—"

Nan started. She might not have recognized the ill-clad boy, but she knew the voice. It was Tim Dykes, whose oldest brother had been transported for poaching. Was he the one—? But her father did not act as if he had his prey to hand, rather as if he expected some information of value.

"Very well, give me the truth, fellow, and I'll keep my part of the bargain. Ten golden boys—" Squire Mallory reached into an inner pocket and brought out a netted purse. He shook it so

there was no mistaking the metallic chime of what lay inside. "Ten golden boys for the truth!"

"I did see 'im, Squire. He be a-hid in the bush like, watchin' the fire. Me, I came up when I heard the shoutin' and all. There he was. No mistakin' 'im—I saw him clear—just a-hid and watchin'."

"And *who* was watching?"

"Him from the inn, Squire, him what thinks he's so big and all—'twas that Chris Fitton."

Squire Mallory laughed. "Watching my barn burn was he? And you didn't see him a-creeping back from lighting that fire now, did you?"

But it would seem Tim was not yet aware of the need to add to his story.

"No, Squire, 'twas already well burnin' when I comes. It just be him watchin'—"

"Tim, I want you to think well about it." Her father clinked the purse again. "Perhaps you saw more. Think well, boy, think well. Get you to the kitchen now. Cook will give you something to cover those ribs of yours. There will be some gentlemen here later, and I'll want you to tell your story to them. So you think some more about what you are going to say."

Tim scuttled out. Nan saw her father smile as he slipped the purse back in his pocket. Then he left also.

He would see that Tim added to his story. Nan knew that as well as if she had heard him urge the boy to do it. And if Tim swore falsely, Chris Fitton would be brought before the Justices. Maybe her father would not dare to sit in the sentencing, not when he was so closely involved. But he could impress both Sir William Lighten and Mr. Rowley Morris. When he mentioned the gentlemen to whom Tim was to tell his tale, Nan was sure that was whom he meant.

The Fittons must be warned. Nan moved from behind the

curtain. There was no one in this house she dared to trust to send a message by; her father ruled with too heavy a hand. Which meant—she would have to go herself. There was the way through the woods which gave on the back of the inn. The snow was coming down, but not too deeply to shut her in as yet. She must move now if she ever was to go. Having made her decision, Nan went about carrying it out.

Cloaked and wearing the heaviest of her shoes, she slipped away from the house to cut across the garden, using the wall there to cover her going, even though that was not the shortest way. So she stumbled on into the woods path, clutching the folds of her cloak more tightly about her.

It got dark early when it snowed. Already, though the hour could not be more than midafternoon, the light was graying fast. She slipped and slid as she went, hurrying so she had a stitch of pain in her side, and she gasped for breath. Then the outer wall of the inn loomed before her, and Nan hesitated.

If she went on openly, rounding the side of the building to the front door, she could not miss being seen. And she did not doubt that news of her visit to the Red Hart would spread through the village, would eventually reach her father's ears. The snow was continuing to fall but not enough to hide her going.

She could, however, see no other way of getting in. After making as sure as she could that there was no one in sight, she flitted across to shelter under the arch of the front door. Luckily that was on the latch, and she could open it without knocking. But she was not sure about the interior as she had never been inside. Where could she find Master Fitton?

The hall she stepped into was hardly warmer than the world outside. Now she could hear voices as she crept along. To her right must lie the taproom, somewhere beyond that the kitchen. Both places would be dangerous for her. She eyed a short side hall, which opened from the foot of the flight of stairs, more impressive-looking even than those at the Manor, and wondered if she dared try any of the closed doors there.

Then she started back, almost ready to retreat to the outer world once more, as one of those doors opened and a man stepped into the dusky hall, carrying a candle in one hand. Nan blinked and knew him—fortune had aided her in this so far. It was Master Fitton himself.

She must have made some sound without realizing it, for his head turned quickly and then he strode toward her.

"What's to do—?" he began.

Nan scraped the hood of her cloak back from her head, so it no longer shadowed her face. On impulse she put her mittened hand up to her mouth, hoping he would understand her warning. He must have, for he glanced over his shoulder at once and then beckoned her forward into the room he had just quitted.

There was a fire on the hearth, and she reached out her hands to it. Now that she was here some of her courage seeped away; she felt shy. How could she tell this man what she feared her father planned?

"Miss Mallory." He spoke her name very quietly. "Why have you come here?"

Yes, he must think it very strange. She must tell him at once, or she would not be able to tell him at all. "My father—he has offered money, a great deal of money, for the name of the one who started the fire."

Ira Fitton nodded, but his face was so grim-set she nearly turned and ran from the room. With a last surge of mingled fear and courage, she gabbled out the rest:

"A boy—Tim Dykes—he came to my father. He says that he saw Chris, your son, in the bushes watching the fire. My father has sent for the others—Sir William Lighten and Mr. Morris. Tim is to tell his story to them. But—" She could not go on, for the rest was a guess, not the truth. How could she tell this stern-looking man that she believed her father would get Tim to lie? Her snow-dampened mittens fell to the floor, and she twisted her cold fingers together tightly.

"Tim Dykes," the innkeeper repeated. "You are sure it was Tim Dykes and not Sampson?"

"Tim!" she repeated vehemently.

Now he was frowning but, Nan thought, not at her, but rather at some thought of his own. Then he looked at her again as if he was really seeing her.

"Miss Mallory, you have done a thing for which we shall be very grateful. Forewarned is forearmed. But by coming here—"

"It's all right," she said hurriedly. "I can go back. I don't think anyone will see me. And I must go alone, you see. Because—"

Again he seemed to understand without her having to put it into words. But he shook his head. "I will go with you to the end of the woods." He stooped and picked up her mittens, giving them back to her.

Though Nan longed to refuse, she guessed that he would not listen to any of her excuses. It seemed to her that she did not breathe freely again until she was safely indoors at the Manor, her damp cloak hidden in the depths of the wardrobe in her own chamber, with the boots pushed under it, and slippers on her cold feet. The snow was falling much faster now, drifting across the garden, already filling in, Nan hoped, her tracks there.

Chris had been seated for a longer time than he could reckon, his books before him, the task Mr. Preston had set him only half begun. He chewed the end of his quill pen and stared out the window where the snow was like a curtain. No one had been near him for what seemed a very long time. He had tried to act as always, though he was sure that rumor had made it plain there was some strain of feeling between his father and himself.

But his thoughts turned mostly to Sampson Dykes. Where had he been last night? He still could not accept the idea that Sam had set the fire. The Dykeses had had it very hard since the Squire turned them out. With Andrew gone, sent off in chains by the Squire, Sam had been left the eldest. Chris knew that Sam hated the Squire, but surely he had sense enough not to get himself into trouble and make things even worse for his mother.

If it were Tim Dykes now—Chris spat a small piece of feather from between his teeth. Tim was as unlike Sam as day from night. He thought Andrew a hero and had talked big about making the Squire pay. Chris squirmed uneasily. That had all been big talk—surely it had!

"Chris—"

The boy started. He had been so deep in thought he had never heard the opening door. "Sir?" He scrambled to his feet to face his father.

"What lies between you and Tim Dykes?"

It was almost as if he had been reading Chris's mind. The boy was so astounded that he spoke the truth without trying to shade it in the favor of the Dykeses.

"Nothing—much. He talks big because he hates the Squire— on account of Andrew. Sam says he always trailed after Andrew. I think, well, I think he takes it unkindly that Sam and I are friends."

Ira Fitton sat down on the edge of the table. "Unkindly enough that he would want to get you into trouble?"

Chris stared blankly at his father. "Why?"

"It has been reported to me, on very good authority, that Tim was up to the Manor and said that he saw you in the bushes watching the fire. We can perhaps believe that by the time he tells his story again something more will be added to it—enough to set you on the spot with a torch in your hand!"

"But I didn't—" Chris began and then gulped. He knew only

too well what his father said was true, and now he was suddenly more afraid than he had ever been in his life.

"This snow is both for and against us"—Ira Fitton had crossed to the small-paned window—"I do not think either Sir William Lighten or Mr. Morris will stir abroad in the storm. But neither will Hawkins be able to get out of London. I greatly doubt we shall see any coaches for a day—maybe more."

"What—what do we do?" Chris asked in a small voice.

"We wait. There is nothing else to be done at present—except that our Jack is listening—carefully—to the village talk. He's my man more than just the groom when it comes to using his ears."

Chris laid down his tooth-mangled quill. Waiting was going to be very hard.

And it was. It was three days before a thin sun melted the road enough to let the coaches through. And for most of the minutes of those three days Chris waited tensely for Squire Mallory to put him under arrest. His father said very little, but twice Jack came stamping in and was closeted in his father's private room. What they talked about Chris did not know, but he felt there was nothing good or surely his father would tell him.

On the fourth day the London coach came squelching over the snow, and Chris made himself useful as ever, running errands, carrying the "house glass" of brandy to each of the four passengers who wanted only the warmth of the common room. That is, three of them did, but the fourth hailed his father and was borne off to the small parlor.

The coach had fresh teams and was off again, three passengers reluctantly taking seats, before Lucy the maid came to Chris with his father's order to join him.

He found the stranger sitting in his father's armchair, his booted feet stretched out to the fire. He was a burly man, lacking Ira Fitton's inches, but very wide of shoulder and thick through

154

the chest. With his capped overcoat hung over the bench by the fire, he showed a blue coat with a yellow waistcoat, both of which looked pale against the ruddy color of his face where the jowls had a pricking of sandy beard.

"So this is the desperate character." He greeted Chris with a voice which echoed around the walls. Then he grinned and winked. Chris did not know just how to take him, though the man's heavy face held an expression of keen interest.

"Now, lad, I want the truth. No holding back, mind you. It's the truth I've got to have to work from. Why were you in the woods that night?"

Chris hesitated. That this was the runner Hawkins, he was now sure. But to tell the whole truth was going to bring Sampson into it— And let Squire Mallory get the hint of Sam's poaching and—

"When Henry Hawkins gives his word"—the man hitched forward a trifle in his chair—"then he means it, lad. Do you have knowledge of who set that fire and think to cover for him?"

"No." Chris was satisfied that he could answer that with the truth.

"Then if you know of some other wrong-doing as has not been spoken of, I shall shut my ears to that part of it—seeing as how I come on one case alone and that as a favor to the Sergeant Major here. Now I ask you again, What was you a-doing in the woods that night?"

"I went to meet someone—" Chris began carefully.

"That someone being another lad as has good reason to hate the Squire."

Chris stared.

"Jack has kept his ears open." His father spoke for the first time. "You went there to meet Sampson Dykes. But he did not come?"

Chris shook his head. "I heard the shouting, and I went to see

155

what was happening—I was in the bushes by the hedge in the long field."

"And you did see someone else?"

Reluctantly Chris told his story: Sampson had not come; Sampson would not have fired the hayrick—that, he repeated over and over. Then he spoke of the voice from the shadow he could not identify.

"Now this Tim as says he saw you, he has something against you?"

"Well—" Once more Chris repeated what he had said to his father concerning Tim.

"And what sort of a lad might he be?"

This time Chris was firm in his head shake. "I—I don't know. He was so mad over what happened to Andrew, his brother Andrew. He and Sam were never ones to see things the same way. Sam, he wanted to get a job, be able to help his mother and the two little ones; he said talking about getting back at the Squire wouldn't do any good."

"And you believed him?"

Chris nodded vigorously.

"And what does Squire Mallory have against you?" Hawkins swung into another track.

"He doesn't like us here at the inn." Chris thought his father must certainly have told Hawkins that already. "And a little while ago Miss Nan—she heard I had a fox cub for a pet. She came riding down to see it. The Squire, he caught me talking to her 'bout it. He was fired up—swung his whip and tried to lay it across me. But I got out of his reach too quick."

Hawkins raised a finger and scratched the stubble on his jaw. "Sounds like a man with a strong temper, this Mallory."

"He's not even gentry," Chris burst out. "Just some cit who made a purseful and bought out Lady Mary when the old Squire took and died and left her with nothing. He wants to lord it over all of us."

"There are that kind," Hawkins remarked. "And powerful enemies they can make themselves, too, lad. Well, we'll see what we can discover as will stop his mouth when it comes to calling the law over you."

What Hawkins proceeded to do, Chris was not sure. He seemed to do nothing but sit in the taproom, listening to any who found their way up from the village for a pint. Being shut in by the snow had made men restless, and now that they could get around, they came into the inn for a bit of company.

But in midafternoon, there was a stir in the courtyard and a thundering knock at the door. Chris was taking a tray of newly washed tankards to the taproom when the door itself was flung open and Squire Mallory strode in, several men at his back, among them Nevison and his two sons.

The Squire pointed with his whip at Chris. "There's the rogue, right to hand. Lay him by the heels, now!"

Chris retreated until his back was against the wood of the hall paneling. But Dolph Nevison and Hal came at him, and before he could defend himself, they had caught his arms. The tray with the tankards crashed to the floor.

What followed was like the wildest of his nightmares. For the sound of the falling tankards brought out his father, and behind him Hawkins and the rest of those in the taproom. The Squire had a pistol, and he shouted that no one was going to rescue this rogue, that if any moved they could be lawfully taken as accomplices.

"Now that"—Hawkins did not raise his voice unduly, but the very force of it overrode the Squire's—"ain't exactly legal, sir. You ain't taking one as was caught in the act, you might say. So where is the warrant whereby you've entered this house?"

"Warrant!" Squire Mallory looked as if he would try either his pistol or his whip on the other. "We've had testimony sworn as to the nature of this gallows-meat and what he did."

From under his arm Hawkins produced a short baton, which glinted in the light from the open door behind. There was a gilt crown on the tip, and this he pushed toward the Squire for the latter's better seeing.

"I am the King's Man, out of Bow Street, called here to clear up this same case."

"Then why isn't this rogue under irons?"

" 'Cause it ain't been established yet as how he's guilty, sir. Now was you to give me your evidence as you say you have—"

Mallory nodded to the door, and Nevison reached behind him dragging into the light the cowering Tim.

"An eyewitness," Mallory said. "Which is as good as any warrant."

"Well enough, sir, but let us all just have it out together—and not in this hall, if you please."

There was something about Hawkins that carried authority, sweeping even the unwilling Squire behind him on into the taproom. They had already lashed Chris's wrists together behind his back, and now the older of the Nevisons took him roughly by the shoulder and shoved him along.

If the Squire had thought to command the action within, he was mistaken, for Hawkins took control as if this sort of proceeding were common and he had done so many times before.

Chris was pushed down on a bench, the younger Nevison on guard, while the Squire took up position with his back to the fireplace, his eyes ever on the move between Ira Fitton and the Bow Street runner, as if he classed them both as his enemies in some duel now to begin. But Hawkins turned to Tim Dykes and in his rumble of a voice began slowly to ask questions as if it did not matter too much. Tim's name, his age, did he have a brother, and finally one which sent Tim silent. What was *he* doing abroad in the woods that night?

After a short pause Tim answered, "I heard all the ado and came runnin'—"

"Now, let's think on that." Hawkins caught him up. "As I have seen it, and I did me a bit of looking around earlier today, this here"—he dipped the end of his baton in the nearest tankard of ale and drew a square to one side—"is the farm where the burning was. And here"—he drew another line—"is the lane what comes up from the village. Do I have it right?"

A chorus of those leaning forward to see the better assured him he did.

"Then here's the place where at young Chris was." He made a spot with a big ale drop. "Now you tell me where *you* were!" He swung suddenly on Tim.

Tim stared down at the table and then looked for a second at Hawkins before dropping his eyes. "I was comin' up from the village like everyone else," he said shrilly.

"But that you couldn't have been. Not if you saw Chris. There is a stand of orchard right here." Once more Hawkins printed a series of dots. "And you couldn't have seen him—not at night. Now could you, lad? Unless you was somewhere's else than that lane—and maybe with someone else—"

"No! I ain't—I weren't—I never was—" Tim looked from one face to another. "All right. Maybe I weren't in the lane, but I saw Chris! Want me to swear it certain, do you, that I do?"

"I'm not denying you might have seen Chris. And he ain't denied to me where he was. Also he heard you— You called his name out, didn't you?"

Tim looked hunted, seemed to shrink smaller. Hawkins leaned farther across the table and pointed his baton at him. "You ain't no match for Harry Hawkins, boy. I've tumbled men as would make you screech your lungs out just to look on. You was there; you called out Chris's name. But there was someone else—now wasn't there? Someone as your calling out that there way hid, getting Chris's attention so that other could creep away all quiet like. There—was—someone—else!" Hawkins said those last four words solemnly, like someone pronouncing sentence.

"I ain't—I ain't going to say—" Tim put up a last defense.

But Hawkins was shaking his head back and forth slowly. "You'll say, lad. You're going to tell me who it was who crept away while you kept Chris Fitton's attention. Now was it your brother?"

"Sam"—Tim half spat the name. "He ain't got the stomach for anything. He's as soft as rabbit fur, he is."

"And who might be hard where Sam is so soft? Might it be Jem Catsby now?"

Tim looked as if Hawkins had struck him across the face. "I ain't said it—I never did!" he half screamed.

"You just did, lad." Hawkins straightened up. "You just did, even if you didn't use the words yourself. You've been mighty close with Jem lately; there's plenty who marked that. And Jem, he takes off innocentlike, for London, he says. Then two nights later, there's a fire. Now who can suspect Jem, who has been hiding out nice and snug, with you to fetch and carry and play lookout for him? Then you come to lie away young Chris's life, and get you and Jem free—"

Tim's thin shoulders shook. "He told me—he said as how it would work fine. We'd get back at the Squire, and no one would know never—"

"There's always them as thinks they can outwit the law," Hawkins said. " 'Course they don't in the end. Well, sir"—he spoke now to the Squire—"you has your man, this Catsby.

Though where he may be now, since he probably took to his heels before the storm, is another matter."

"You're Fitton's friend—" the Squire began. Hal Nevison reached down and sawed through the cords binding Chris. Hal's father looked at Ira Fitton. "Ira, I listened to—"

The innkeeper shook his head. "I know what moved you, Henry. Don't let it trouble you. It's all right now the truth is known. And it is known." He stared straight at the Squire.

Mallory's thin mouth worked as if he were cursing silently. Then he flung out of the room, the Nevisons following.

Hawkins looked at Tim. "It seems that they forgot you, lad. Now before they remember too much and maybe come a-looking to make it hot for you, best get the law on your side. You tell me all you know about this Catsby, and we'll see if we can't forget that you had too big a part in his Devil's work."

Chris leaned back against the wall; he felt weak and tired and so thankful that he could not find the words he knew he owed Hawkins and his father. He only knew that he was free of a burden he had been carrying.

8 "Your Word Against Theirs"

Chris opened his eyes. This time he was not surprised to see overhead the ceiling of the room in Aunt Elizabeth's apartment instead of the years-darkened wood of the inn. He did not move at first, just lay thinking of the scene from which he had come by some means he could never understand. The fear which had held him so strongly as he sat with bound hands and listened to Hawkins' careful questioning of Tim was gone.

But he had been left with a want to know more. What had happened to Tim? And had they ever caught Catsby? He thought mostly about Hawkins and about his father—the Ira Fitton of the inn, the father who had believed in him and had then moved to do the best he could for his son.

Chris could close his eyes and see that other's face as if Sergeant Major Fitton stood in this very room here and now. A queer sense of loss crept in to fill the emptiness which fear had left. In spite of all that had happened to him, had threatened him this time within the walls of the Red Hart, he longed to be back there.

"Chris!"

There had come a cautious tap at the door; his name was called in a voice hardly above a whisper. He wriggled out of bed. What did Nan want? It was very early yet; the light was gray.

"What is it?" His answering whisper sounded like a hiss.

"Chris—you *are* here then—"

Now what in the world did *that* mean? Chris opened the door a crack. Nan pushed it farther open, enough for her to slip in.

"You—you're all right?"

"Why shouldn't I be?"

"I thought—the Squire—he was going to take you. I heard him talking to the Nevisons. I didn't know what was going to happen!"

"You were there then? But I didn't see you, not this time!"

She held her robe closer about her as if she were cold, though the bedroom was so warm after the remembered ever-present chill of the inn that Chris felt nearly too hot.

"I was a Nan again, too, a different one though. Sometimes I wonder— Was I once all those Nans? This time I went down to the inn. I told your father about Tim, about what the Squire might try to do. My father wanted Tim to change his story; he offered him the money to say he saw you actually setting fire to the rick. What happened, Chris? Did Tim lie?"

"He didn't get a chance." Chris swept a pile of clothing off the chair and motioned Nan to sit down. "Hawkins fixed him, but good."

Nan listened so eagerly that Chris found himself describing the scene at the inn with more detail than he planned. When he ended with the departure of the Squire, she looked disappointed. "That was all?"

"Oh, Hawkins said something about Tim's helping with more facts and so making it easier for himself. But—it all seemed so easy, Nan, when Hawkins laid it out so they could see—drawing up the plan which proved Tim couldn't have been where he said he was, and finding out about Tim and Catsby being so close. Easy—when you know how to do it."

The happiness was gone from Chris's face now. He had that shut-in sullen look again.

"Chris," she ventured, "what's the matter? It came right in the dream, didn't it?"

"This isn't the dream," he returned flatly.

"You *are* in trouble."

At first he resented Nan's statement. It was no business of hers. Who was she? Then memory returned; there were a number of Nans now he could think of. There was the Nan who by a trick had helped him save Master Bowyer; there was the Nan who had led him to warn the dragoons; there was that last Nan—he had no doubt that she had done exactly as she had just now told him, carried the news of Tim to his father so both Ira Fitton and Harry Hawkins had been forewarned as to what weapon the Squire held. Then there was *this* Nan. When he looked directly at her, one face seemed to fit over another until they became the one he knew best.

"I'm in trouble." And because he could not see any way that he could fight this time, he told her of his attempt to outwit Canfield and what had come of it.

"So there are two questions which were the same." She sat up very straight in the chair, her hands folded in her lap. "But, Chris, if you had been selling the whole exam, the way they said, then all the questions would be the same, wouldn't they?"

"They can say I was doing it for money," he pointed out.

"There has to be some way you can prove it," she said hotly. On her face was the same look of determination he had seen two of those other Nans wearing. Her chin was up and her eyes were bright with beginning anger. Not against him, Chris realized with a small odd shock, but *for* him! Nan was ready to help.

"I don't know how."

"This Mr. Battersley, how well do you know him, Chris?"

"Not much better than I know any of them." For the first

time he allowed a crack to open in his shell against the world. "I hate the place! Battersley's tough, but he's fair. And he knows his stuff. I got pretty good marks on my papers so far this term."

"And Canfield and the rest?"

"They aren't in my section. That's the point. I have that class before they do, so it'd be easy to slip along information about the exam."

"Then why go to all the bother of making up questions," Nan pointed out. "And the wrong questions?"

"They say it's for the money."

Nan considered the point. There must be some chink in Canfield's argument—there had to be. But it was not going to be as easy to find as the weak point in the Squire's accusation had been. That had been built on a lie, and one easily overturned by a man used to questioning liars and ready to expect some sort of cover-up.

"Can they prove you need money?"

Chris looked thoughtful. "I don't see how they can, but, of course, one can always use money. I showed Aunt Elizabeth my wallet. I've two dollars left from my allowance—that's all. But they can say I hid it somewhere."

"It's your word against theirs then—"

"That's just the point, you see. They're big—or at least Canfield is. He's captain of the soccer team, and his gang will back up what he tells them. I'm a loner—"

"You are *you*," Nan said quietly; and something in the way she looked at him made Chris feel queer, as if she believed he could do just about anything he wanted to—beginning with taking on the whole Academy. Except that was impossible, of course.

"I'd go to Mr. Battersley," she continued. "Your best argument is the fact that the exams don't agree. How many questions were there anyway, Chris?"

"Six. But—" He shook his head slowly. "I can't blab to the Batman that I was so afraid of being roughed up that I made all this up. It's the disgusting truth"—he made himself say that—"but it's one I'm not going to tell."

"Has anyone ever done this before—sold exams, I mean?" Nan was off now on another tack.

Chris shrugged. "I don't know. At least no one ever told me about it. I've only been there this one term anyway."

"It sounds to me," Nan said slowly, "as if this Canfield had an answer ready because he expected some trouble. Just like Pat—"

"Pat who?"

Nan gave him a quick, uncomfortable glance. And then made up her mind swiftly. Maybe if she showed him he was not the only one— She told her story of the "shopping" trip in a few sentences which did not spare her own ignorance.

"But you did it!" Chris nodded. "You got them off your back! Only I can't use your gimmick—it wouldn't work. This is not the same thing at all."

"I did it," Nan remembered, "because I thought about Uncle Jasper—and how I was able to trick him. Chris, you did things which were brave. You went for the dragoons, and you told the truth to the Bow Street runner so he was able to save you. There's got to be a way—"

"Those—I was dreaming!"

"I wonder." Nan got up from the chair and went to pick up the inn. For the first time she had no feeling of discomfort as she handled it. When she set it back on the night table, she brushed an envelope to the floor. Hurriedly she picked it up.

"That's mine!" Chris snatched it from her with some of his old hostility.

But Nan dared to answer him this time. "That's from your father—and you never even read it."

Chris's scowl was blacker than she had ever seen it. He

twisted the envelope between his fingers as if he would tear it apart unopened. Then, with a defiant glance at her, he ripped it open and spread out the typewritten sheet it contained.

At least, thought Nan bleakly, he gets a letter; I get postcards. Just then she did not know whether she envied Chris or not.

"Chris—Nan—"

Aunt Elizabeth! Nan hurried to the door and peeped through the crack she allowed to open there. Aunt Elizabeth must be calling from the kitchen. Without a backyard look she went across to her own room and started hurriedly to dress.

Chris read the letter. So *they* were coming home—and Dad had a surprise he was sure would suit Chris. Well, Chris had had enough of Dad's surprises. He crumpled the page in one hand and glanced at the inn. For a moment he wished once more he was back there—with Sergeant Major Fitton, who perhaps did not go in for surprises but who was satisfyingly *there* when someone needed him.

He set about dressing. Nan had meant well, he would admit that, but nothing she had said was of very much help. He would have to go to the Academy with Aunt Elizabeth and face them all with only his own word. And to Chris at that moment that seemed of very little worth indeed.

Aunt Elizabeth made a lot of cheerful talk which he did not listen to through breakfast nor even in the taxi she had ordered. They were both to be dropped off at the Academy, and Nan was then to go on to school alone. Chris, remembering Nan's story of how she had confronted Pat and Marve, wriggled on the seat. But she had had a good out. He wished for a moment or two he had Harry Hawkins instead of Aunt Elizabeth here beside him, the comfort of that deep rolling voice in his ears instead of the light chatter which was so disturbing.

As they went into the Academy, he caught sight of Canfield up ahead. There was a man with him. Canfield's father? Were

they going to drag everyone's family into this? Chris did not let himself turn and run as he wanted to, but the hopeless depression within him grew darker and darker.

It was not the Headmaster who sat in the office—though it was his office. Mr. Battersley occupied the chair behind the desk there, rising to greet both Aunt Elizabeth and Mr. Canfield, who wore an impatient expression.

Chris sat on the edge of the hard chair. He did not glance at Canfield. But he did meet the Batman's gaze and held it until the man looked over to where Canfield must be.

"I have been asked to conduct this meeting"—Mr. Battersley's dry, emotionless tone could cover anything; it was well known that you could not shake the Batman—"since it is in my class this matter began. I have had your story, Canfield—"

"It's perfectly plain what happened"—that was Mr. Canfield cutting in.

A single lift of the Batman's eyebrows seemed enough to dry up that fuming voice. "Fitton"—Chris looked stolidly back at the Batman—"I presume you have been told what this is all about."

"They say I sold the copies of the test."

"Not *the* test—a test," Mr. Battersley corrected. "There are two similar questions. The rest—I am interested by this, Fitton—where did you get the others? Oddly enough they are perfectly legitimate questions based on this semester's work. But they are not ones I considered using this time, nor have I used them in the past. I must believe that you yourself concocted them?" He made that a question instead of a statement.

"Yes," Chris answered with the flat truth.

"Enterprising of you. Now"—the Batman's gaze went to Canfield—"you have told me that Fitton approached you and offered to sell you a set of exam questions. Since your class record is anything but distinguished, you agreed to his proposi-

Red Hart Magic

tion. He supplied you with a carbon which you proceeded to share with certain friends, until Mr. Powers saw what was going on and confiscated the papers and sent you to me. You then admitted what happened and said that the idea was Fitton's and you had each paid him five dollars for the use of the carbon. Am I correct in stating what you claim as facts?"

"The little double-crosser! He never meant to give us the real thing—he was too yellow to get it!" Canfield was seething.

"Fitton?" Again Mr. Battersley swung back to him.

Canfield was no Tim Dykes confronted by the force of the law and fear of those questioning him. But the way Mr. Battersley had expressed that, his choice of words— Dare Chris believe the Batman still had an open mind and he was not already convicted? He must do the best he could—just as Hawkins had done his best at the inn.

"I made up the questions," he said. "That much is right. But I did not sell them."

"Just what was your purpose, Fitton? To make trouble generally?"

"They said they wanted questions—I went over what we'd had in class and gave them an exam. I wasn't going to take the real one—"

"Ah." Mr. Battersley put the fingers of his hands together, erecting a "steeple." "You interest me, Fitton. So it was suggested that you obtain the exam for the benefit of others?"

"That's a lie!" Canfield's voice was high and shrill. "He came to us. It was all his idea!"

"You made some very revealing remarks earlier, Canfield when you referred to the fact that Fitton was "too yellow," as you termed it, to get the real examination. If he approached you *after* he had supposedly stolen my papers, why would you have that vehement reaction?"

170

"Now look here," Mr. Canfield cut in, "so the kid got suckered in by this Fitton. He'll admit he did that much, but you have no right to imply that he put Fitton up to it in the first place."

Mr. Battersley paid no attention; instead he looked directly at Chris once more. "Were you approached to steal the exam?"

"Yes."

"Did you accept money for this?" He twitched the sheet lying on the desk before him.

"No."

"He's a liar! Ask Jimmy Baxter—Harvey—DeTenbus—" flared Canfield.

Again Mr. Battersley paid no heed to that interruption to his questioning.

"This examination represents a lot of complicated work. It could only have been done by someone who had a driving purpose. You admit that you did it, Fitton; now I am going to ask you why?"

Chris knew there was no escape; he had been driven into a corner, and truth was the only way out. But suddenly, as it had come to him in the inn when he knew that no lie could ever serve and that he must face himself as he was, he answered, "Because I was afraid."

Those four words fell into a silence which grew more awful as every second ticked away. But he had said them, and they were the truth.

"I am not going to ask you of what you were afraid, Fitton—oddly enough I don't believe that you are any more." The precise voice reached Chris with the same authority that Harry Hawkins' strong rumble had carried.

"This matter must go to the Headmaster and I do not know what his decision will be. I shall make my own report. However,

I am convinced of one thing; this was not done for any gain. Canfield"—he made that name snap like a whip—"you never gave any money to Fitton. Now, did you?"

There was a silence as deep as before.

"I—" It was as if Canfield had tried and failed.

"At least you have not lied yourself in any deeper. I will tell you now that Harvey Reed has admitted that no money was passed. And the rest of *his* story differs quite a bit from what you told me yesterday. You did not pick your confederates very well, it would seem. But for the rest—it is entirely up to Dr. Stevens."

Chris drew an uncertain breath. He did not know whether what he felt was relief or not; he certainly could not be as sure of the future as he had been when the Bow Street runner had taken charge. But today it had been his word against theirs—and Mr. Battersley had believed him. And the Batman had been right, too: Chris was not afraid any more. Canfield had shrunk—he was no longer a dictator who had full control over Chris's well-being.

He heard Mr. Canfield still protesting. Aunt Elizabeth, for once, had said nothing at all, to both Chris's surprise and relief. Now she might even be ready to find her tongue again. But none of that mattered. He did not even care that he would have to face Dr. Stevens and might even be kicked out of the Academy. Nothing mattered except that he had said he was a coward—and then had found out that it was not true! A sudden warmth filled him. It was like standing before the fire on the inn hearth out of the freezing chill of the winter night. Because he had never faced up to his fears before, he had twisted and tried to evade, told himself he just wasn't going to be drawn into anything. Because he did not want to face himself as the timid coward he was—or had thought he was.

And was no longer. Nan had told him—the inn had told him—and now he knew.

9 A Family–Maybe

"What happened?"

Nan came into the apartment as if she had been running a race. Chris looked up from his book.

"I got suspended—for the rest of the week, or until Dr. Stevens makes up his mind."

"But they believed you!" That was no question, rather a statement.

"The Batman did." Chris did not want to talk about it; he had heard enough from Aunt Elizabeth. Yet—he owed Nan this. Slowly he described that sorry scene in the office; at least he saw it as a sorry one. He still cringed inside whenever he thought of admitting that he was afraid—afraid of Canfield and his gang.

"You weren't afraid"—Nan broke in swiftly as if she could read his thoughts—"at least not so much afraid you couldn't say so. You—you were braver than I was. I should have taken that pin back to the counter—told them everything. But—*then* I couldn't."

Chris eyed her curiously. "You say, *then* you couldn't. Why?"

"Because now I think I could." She laid her book bag down and flopped into the chair nearby. "I never told Grandma things—not really. Because I was always afraid I would disappoint her, and then maybe she wouldn't like me so much.

And she was the only one I had. So"—she drew a deep breath—"when Grandma wasn't here, I felt I didn't really have anybody. Only, you don't really need others to tell you what is right and what is wrong. You *know* it somehow—inside you know it.

"I knew that Uncle Jasper was using me to do bad things to people who trusted me. I knew that Aunt Prudence was doing right when she wouldn't let the smugglers get your father—" Nan plunged on.

His father—Chris remembered that fever-flushed face on the thin pillow in the inn bed. It was a stranger's face now, but he could remember the fear and the anger that had filled him then.

"And I knew that the Squire was going to use a lie to hurt you—so I—that time I was strong enough to go and tell. Though I was afraid all the time I did it. If he had found out—" Nan paused and shivered. "I wonder if he ever did find out and what happened to that other Nan. I hope he never did. Never!"

"So do I!" Chris surprised himself by saying. And then he added more slowly:

"You know, I've always felt alone. There was always just one—me. Dad was away all the time—I'd be shipped around. Once to Uncle Pete's. They didn't really want me—you sure can tell. And then here. And I thought maybe—when I got old enough not to be a bother the way a little kid is—then Dad would want me."

He was hardly aware he was telling Nan things he had locked inside until the hurt never quite faded away. It was as if some gag had been torn from his mouth, so that now he could not stop that flood even if he wanted to.

"Dad would send money. *Money!* But—"

"But he didn't come himself," Nan finished for him softly when Chris did not continue. "But you got letters. Maybe he couldn't help it."

174

"It was like—" Chris shook his head. "I don't know—like we were talking different languages—even when he came. He'd ask questions as if he didn't know just what to say. I'd save up things to tell him, but I never did. There was a dad I thought I knew, but when he came, that was never him."

"I was luckier." Nan was not looking at him but staring at the thick carpet. "I had Grandma for a while. But it's true—mostly, I guess, I was just one, too. Like I was one with Uncle Jasper, and with Aunt Prudence, and when I was Miss Mallory. It's awfully lonely being just one."

"I wasn't one," Chris burst out to interrupt her, "not at the inn, I wasn't! I wish, I wish I could go back."

Nan sat up quickly, gazing at him with a kind of fear. "No! Chris, you have to be yourself—Not those other Chrises—the self that is here! If you try—that is running away. I don't know if you could—but it is running. Don't ever, ever try!"

"You think I could do it?"

"You mustn't try!" Nan was begging him now. "You must never try! I have a feeling, truly, I do, Chris, that that would be wrong. You would lose the real you and never, never find yourself again if you do that."

"I would rather not be the one I am now."

"We would all rather not be ourselves sometimes," Nan said slowly. "But we have to be. I don't like myself much at times. I didn't like what I did for Uncle Jasper—it was horrible! And sometimes I do things like that now. Oh, I don't mean listen to people and then tell soldiers what they are doing. But I don't always stand up for what I believe is right. Not the way Aunt Prudence did. Not the way you did, Chris."

He laughed scornfully. "I'm no prize. I told you, I'm no hero."

"You don't have to be a hero—just Chris Fitton as he's always been."

Now he stared at her. "You, you got something you— No, don't keep thinking that about me!" He got up and went to stand looking out of the apartment window, his back shutting her out.

But Nan refused to be shut out. Whenever she looked at Chris, those other Chrises seemed to melt in and become a part of him. She did not see the usually sullen-faced boy she had—yes, she thought, she had hated him then. It was all a part of the breakup of her calm and peaceful life with Grandma. The inn had forced her to act more positively than she had ever believed she could. It had proved something to her. Now she was certain that one could change inside. It would be hard work, and she would probably try to dodge other choices, she knew that—because she was still the person she had been. But she was not going to *stay* that person, and she would fight all the way, fight the fear and the loneliness, and the wanting to be more than "just one."

"I am going to remember all those Chrises," she said now quietly. "And maybe you'll remember those Nans. The other ones who could do things—the right things—"

Chris swung around. "I didn't want you for a sister," he said abruptly. "I didn't want you here—" He paused; it was hard to choose the right words now. "I—Aunt Elizabeth said we were all a family now. I didn't believe that."

She was nodding. "I didn't either," she answered him promptly, so promptly and with such empathy that he was a little shaken. He had so long only considered—and tried to keep hidden—his own feelings that it was startling to know his dislike had been reflected by her.

"All right. Maybe we were both wrong." The words were twisted out of him. All his runaway speech of a few minutes before was fast drying up. "We can start over—" He made that effort, and it *was* an effort.

"I'm willing," Nan returned.

Chris came slowly away from the window. "I'm not good at making friends," he warned her.

"I never had any—close ones—except Grandma. So I'm not either."

"Wait!" Chris had a sudden inspiration. He hurried out of the room.

Wait for what? Nan wondered. She stared at the tips of her shoes where they scuffed up the long pile of the carpet and thought about Chris. Hard to be friends? She was not quite sure that she could be one—not a real friend. Oh, she had known girls and gone around with them back in Elmsport and called them friends. But she had never shared with any of them what she had shared with Chris—those strange too real dreams and what they had said so openly just minutes before. She felt that she knew Chris, the real Chris, better than she knew anyone— maybe even Grandma—now.

And would the time come when Chris would resent her knowing? Nan thought about that in turn. It could be true. But that would be another thing she must learn to face when it came—if it came. No more hiding away from things that must be faced.

Chris came banging back into the room. He was carrying the inn, and now he stood directly before her, setting the tiny building down on the edge of the coffee table. It was so real, even in its smallness, one might be looking at it through the wrong end of a magnifying glass, one which made things look smaller instead of larger. She half expected to see Aunt Prudence peering out of one of the diamond-paned windows, or a coach pulling through the archway into the courtyard.

"People swear on things," Chris said. "They use Bibles to

177

swear on in court—when they say they are telling the truth. All right, we'll swear on the Red Hart, swear we'll give each other a chance to be friends!"

Nan no longer felt that strange feeling of discomfort and fear which had been hers when she had first seen the inn. Now it was as familiar, and somehow as welcoming to her, as had been the old house at Elmsport. She did not know why they had dreamed and had spent such troubling hours in it. No, they could not have been in *this!* But had Chris not said that models were often made of real ships or planes—and perhaps, too, of houses? Was there a *real* Red Hart and perhaps one day could she and Chris find it?

"Do you swear?" Chris's tone was impatient, drawing her back to the here and now.

"Yes, I do." Nan put out her hand to lay two fingertips on the roof of the inn. "I swear I want to be friends."

Chris was right behind her making the same promise. Then he added, "Might not be too easy—sometimes."

Nan smiled. "Yes. But we can keep trying. We can even be a family—maybe."

Chris looked very thoughtful. Then, as he picked up the inn and balanced it on the flat of his palm at eye level as if he hoped to see something within, he said, "Might not be bad at that. And I think we'll have a chance to prove it. Dad wrote about a surprise—"

"So did Mother," Nan interrupted.

"Could be," Chris considered thoughtfully, "we're just going to have a real home."

He gazed at the Red Hart. In a way, that had been home. He wondered if any other would be as welcoming. There again, they would have to try. He looked at Nan, and for the first time the sullenness was gone from his face, and he smiled. Tentatively, then openly, she smiled back.

About the Author

Andre Norton, who has long had an interest in legends and history, has written many science-fiction and fantasy stories, which have been published both in the United States and in many countries abroad. At one time a children's librarian and bookshop owner, she now devotes her full time to writing, and has been the recipient of various writing and science-fiction awards. Born in Cleveland, Ohio, she lives in Maitland, Florida.

About the Artist

Donna Diamond's beautiful pen-and-ink drawings perfectly exemplify her belief that fantasy is best expressed through carefully rendered detail. A graduate of Boston University's School of Fine and Applied Art, Ms. Diamond has also studied at the Tanglewood Summer Art Program, the High School of Music and Art, and the School of Visual Arts in New York City. In addition to art, she is also interested in the dance, which she has studied and still enjoys watching. She is married to a musician, and lives in New York City.